L. Farnsv

In the Shadow of Prometheus

A Story From the Ring Saga

with Illustrations by John Sumrow
and Cover Design by Raven Gill

Produced in association with Pierce & Partum
www.pierceandpartum.co.uk

For more information, go to www.theringsaga.com
L. Farnsworth can be reached there, and at
lfcolson@theringsaga.com

Reference materials for cataloging—

Colson, L. Farnsworth, 1992—author

*In the Shadow of Prometheus; or, Philosophical
Fragments of an Improbable Future / L. Farnsworth Colson*

A story from the *Ring Saga* series

ISBN 978-1-796-302905

For Kieren Munson-Burke

Contents

Contents (continued)

What this book is all about

It is no great secret that *In the Shadow of Prometheus* is first and foremost a philosophical novel. What does that mean? It means that the author believes that the purpose of literature is to convey insight about the world in which we exist, the struggle of the human condition, and the journey of meaning-making for a life well-lived.

This puts me in direct opposition to the morays of contemporary mass-media publishing, which holds as its theory of marketing that it must give us entertainment to beguile and fascinate us, whatever the social cost. This approach is starkly misaligned with the mentality of the literary greats of our past. As Goethe notably remarked, we need stories which charm humankind, and *edify us too*. Such tales are in woefully short supply these days, which is why I decided to write *Prometheus*.

By consequence, you will notice that many of my influences lie less with modern fiction and more with foundational works in philosophy and religion. For those of you who know me well, this makes perfect sense — my training at Yale was in the philosophy of religion.

Hold up! Before you run away at the very sound of such a profession, please know that I am not a dogmatist, or strictly-speaking even 'religious' or 'spiritual'. But there are texts worth reading in each tradition, and from a historical perspective — religion informs philosophy, which informs science, which informs all of our present world culture. Rather than fixating on civilization's current state, I look to our legacy and the ways it can and will continue to inform our future.

So what is *In the Shadow of Prometheus* all about? It imagines a futuristic and fantastical representation of our world in which the modern nation-state collapses, and in its place is a society which predicates authority on two foundations over the political peacocking of our present-day — those new standards being intellectual authority, and ethical review. It looks at the ways in which human nature might interact with such a model for better and worse, and layers on top of this narrative pedagogy in philosophy and religion to help the reader develop the analytical tools necessary to make sense of all that is being said.

My book is not meant to be an easy read. If you want something to merely distract or amuse you: there's Netflix for that, and hey, I'm all about some quality time for fun narratives like *Stranger Things*. But if you're tired of continuing to walk through life without answers or understanding on these important topics, *In the Shadow of Prometheus* may just be what you've been waiting for.

Acknowledgements

Behind every book is an unseen and under-appreciated network of people who uplift and support its author(s). Therefore, it is the duty of every writer of sound conscience to sing the praises of these persons far and wide, so that their readership might know the whole effort which goes into making a project such as this.

First, I would be remiss if I did not begin with the woman who was with me every step of the way during the creation of this manuscript. Kieren Munson-Burke, I love you. Thank you for being wonderful, and for loving me in kind. You've spent many hours by my side as this story took shape, and I am certain that it would not exist without the positivity with which you nourished my heart over this last year. If nothing else, let this book stand as a testament to the strength of our love and the warmth of our commitment to one another. You are my rock. Thank you for everything.

Next, I want to say thank you to all of my early readers, who gave thoughtful feedback, kind encouragement, and indefatigable support. In particular, I must thank Marjorie Holcombe, who doubtless gave up many other books to stick with my process throughout the entire project, lending me her consistent, helpful insights and observations along the way. In addition, I want to thank April Smith Spencer, Cedric Chanthaboune, Rob E. Champney, and RJ Hale for their friendship as I endeavored to complete this task.

A note on friendship: there are certain people in my life without whom I simply would not be here. Their love and companionship have seen me through the impossible at several points in my life. In no particular order, I want to thank Blair Booth, Michael McCarthy, Tim Kuhn, Robbie Laughton, Sam Friedman,

Kerri Norris, Scott McLeavy, Nathan Gray, Stephen Buckley, Kyle O'Brien, Abigail Gill, Chris Abel, and Calvin Park. When I couldn't run, I walked, and when I couldn't walk, you carried me. I love you all very much.

I want to give special acknowledgement to a pupil of mine who has shown exceptional acuity of thought and depth of insight. They are a bold thinker, a warm companion, and a budding philosopher in their own right. Now it must be said — where I am Freudian, they are Jungian. Where I am analytical, they are mystical. And yet I could not be prouder of their intellectual growth. Jhivan Abdul, it has been a pleasure to mentor you in the study of philosophy. While our time working together was far too short, I hope that it served you well, and that you keep working to cultivate your remarkable mind.

I was very fortunate in this process to run across the good favor of marvelous production talent —

Eliza VanCort brought me from total ignorance about the world of ethical and authentic marketing into something like competence: a monumental achievement which could only ever have been accomplished by a master of the art form.

Raven Gill, a longtime friend, designed the immaculate cover art of this book, which pays deft homage to Wittgenstein's *Investigations* and the aesthetic tastes of the avant-garde of Modern philosophy in the 20th century.

And of course, John Sumrow's iconic additions for each chapter cannot be ignored. I am endlessly in awe of his craft and have enjoyed our fruitful collaboration tremendously. Hopefully this is just the beginning!

My former undergraduate advisor Nicholas Germana was a spectacular mentor and is undeniably the person most responsible for shaping my intellectual development 'in the early years'. Gabriel Citron, Eliyahu Stern, Hannan Hever,

Karsten Harries, and John E. Hare were also very helpful guides during my time in the Academy. I am not sure that this book does any of them justice, but nonetheless I am eager to give them my thanks.

Some ideas in this manuscript were first borne out in unpublished papers submitted to these scholars while under their mentorship. Though the guiding concepts of *Prometheus* remain my own intellectual contribution, the supervision of these brilliant academicians was undoubtably formative.

To my brother Adam, and my mother Sarah: I love you more than words can ever tell. And to my stepfather Clifford: you are a marvel. Thank you for all the wonderful years of humor and wit. I hope some of it spilled into these pages!

My grandfather Willard Colson's life has been far more interesting than any story I could ever write. Nevertheless, he has been wonderfully generous in sharing a part of it with me, and for that I am blessed. He will always be with me in my heart.

Michael, Kim, and Jordan Mirana Munson-Burke — you have been so kind and welcoming to me. Thank you for bringing me into your household and treating me like another one of the pack. I love you all so much.

During the production of this manuscript, my dear friends Tristan and Caitlin welcomed new life into their lives. To their newborn son, George Lincoln Benedict: welcome to the world! We are so happy you have joined us. And always remember — your family is your treasure. Hold it close, child. Mom and dad abound with love, and they will give of themselves like waves from an ocean for whatever is worthwhile in this life. Trust them with your heart and it will *always* be cherished.

To the doubtless many I have failed to mention: I am sorry for it! Please let me know so I can do you justice in later works.

Just such a drama
let us now compose
plunge boldly into life
its depths disclose

Each lives it
not to many it is known
t'will interest wheresoever
seiz'd and shown

bright pictures
but obscure their meaning
a ray of truth
through error gleaming

Thus you the best elixir brew
to charm mankind
and edify them too

— Goethe's *Tragedy of Faust*

Chapter One

§1A

The snow felt like burning cinders tumbling from the height of the mountain. Corvin smiled. He could not fathom what conjured that emberous thought. The biting cold of the Himalayan freeze was a strange backdrop for this inverse imaginary, and although his chest lay bare against the harsh climate—the pain of it was an old acquaintance.

Yet just when the notion seemed as if it were to float away on the tail of a winter's wind, his attention came into focus once more, affixing his gaze on the flickering eyes of a pale leopard with a desperate temper. There was fire there; a spark which would ignite unseen possibilities—this much he knew.

Corvin clenched his fist tightly, the ball of which creaked and trembled under the strength of his grasp. Driblets of blood seeped from superficial marks which were freshly cut along the length of his arm. He let out a modulated sigh, bracing himself for the task at hand.

"Be thankful mortal," a voice called out from within the dark, "the last of your kind to pay homage to Ourself was a serpent, who ate his own tail in order to attest the depth of his sacrifice for Us. Bear these wounds as a mercy, and strike with the urgency of your purpose here."

The shadow from which the call emanated seemed fundamentally familiar to Corvin, like an all-present force of nature—as cardinal to the order of the World as the prominential facade of the mountain which bore its weighty earth beside the beast and he.

The leopard had been docile up until the moment he'd wounded it. Corvin felt fleeting shame as this too came to him, and yet—there was an instinctual energy which permeated the oxygen between them, as though the cold itself were lightning. Despite all misgivings, he saw an ancient destiny in the moment; that the stories which first told it were carved into the distant suns which shown their antediluvian light along the snowed and hallowed ground of the outcrop on which they now stood.

But it was the pale blue of the moonlight which illuminated the twitching of his chest and shoulders, the distress bound up in the furling of his brow, and the beleaguerment of every step he took towards the animal. It was a moment for stoic and reverent silence, and in what followed, only the wind would cry heresy.

The leopard pounced. Corvin, though dazed, could feel the euphoria rush through him as he struck. The creature let out a sonorous howl as its jawline snapped like a branch torn from desiccated birch. In the poor light, its blood seemed to flake like mica stone. Pale and reeling, the leopard sought its distance with frantic urgency.

"Excellent!" the shadow cried, "yet how will you finish what you have begun?"

The reply was a weary exhale at first, though off the tufts of frigid condensation, the necessary words crystallized. "I haven't a choice,

Shadow. You have brought me here for this purpose, and it shall be accomplished. I know what I must do."

"No." said the shadow, "this thought is an illusion, flesh thing. Choice is what animates you. Your eyes deceive you, and your mind consents. Are humans really so weak? Are you truly able to be governed by a mere symbol of things?"

The wounded cat sprang out towards an alcove at the furthest visage of the mountainside. Still much swifter than Corvin, it reached the recess of the granite rock, skirting aside a film of frost as it wheeled to regain sight of its oppressor.

"I've come too far to walk away empty-handed." answered Corvin, "You said the relic requires the blood of its guardian. Here, at the helm of its tomb, a snow-leopard—most sacred of creatures—waits like a watchdog. Do not ask me to acquiesce the destiny that you have revealed for me, for long have we journeyed."

Stepping along the pale scattered dust between him and his fate, Corvin felt his chest soaring, pacing, drumming to the force of each step. The fatal'd creature let out a horrible cry, fragmented between the threads of hisses and turgid breaths.

Wrangling its limbs in a blinding jaunt, the leopard slid against the crook of Corvin's hand. Gliding under his reach, the cat sank its teeth deep into the skin of his forearm, dismantling the clenched fist underneath it into unspoken signs of the subconscious. Shock. Pain. Loss of control. Corvin could feel the fang grazing against the bone and tendon, jostling the fiber of his mother's womb.

He took several deep breaths before roaring, half between humor and pain. "How unfortunate for you, friend." said Corvin, "I have blunted your weapon 'ere you could wield it." He slapped the creature's bloodied chin. It screeched, dislodging its grasp.

Corvin was a tower of darkness, his arm like a drawbridge as he unleashed one final blow. "Rest now, little one." he bellowed, "the quiet winter calls you home."

Wind rippled through the fur of the lifeless figure. The beautiful creature had collapsed in a fetal stance along the contours of the shadow of the alcove. Half-buried in snow, the leopard lay ready.

He cupped the sullied fur of its jaw in his hand. Were it not for a profound and stoic composure, the sight might well have been a father with his child.

Sitting, Corvin pulled the boots from off his feet. He unstrung thick laces from each one, and then used them to bind up the leopard. Corvin's brow unfurled as he came to rest the body against his knee. Raising the creature's empty eyes to his, he sighed once more and gazed upon the cost.

Roping his arms underneath the shoulders of this fragile body, he raised it over his shoulder and walked to the far end of the alcove with his wrist turned so as not to stain its silver coat with the blood of its jaw, which now rested in the crook of his neck. Even the wind fell silent now.

Further past the ridge-line, he found an opening in the body of the mountain. After twenty feet of stone, Corvin emerged into a massive ice-rimmed caldera, in the middle of which stood a gargantuan bodhi tree with great purple crescents growing out of each branch.

The trunk was knotted like a braid along the length of its grain and encased an arm-sized block of stone above it, protruding from the wood at about a fathom's length.

Along each strand of the wooden plait was an engraving bearing strange lettering, the likes of which Corvin had never seen. He paused, gesturing to the shadow. "You question that I could ever be ruled by a symbol. Here I am, unsure of what these ones even mean... and yet they too give me pause. Am I really such a fool?"

"No, not a fool," the voice replied, "just mortal, which is why we are here. Do not worry about these letters. They are a symbol of your destiny, flesh-thing. No more harmful than the constellations which acclaim you. They are a marker for beings like me, not something with which the likes of you need be concerned in the here and now. Claim the purchase, and clean the blood from your hands."

Corvin laid the body behind him and stepped into the nest of roots which reached to the world beyond. He raised his hand against the braid and stained its grain with the price.

At first there was nothing, but then the knotting coiled tightly into a single bar, and the top end—writhing—snaked over the whole of the stone until its dense weight was sealed in the staff's branching grasp. The resulting maul fell weightily into Corvin's hands.

"Is this it?" Corvin asked, "You said I would find my destiny here."

"Well," the shadow replied, "now you will."

The floor of the caldera shattered into veins of molten rock, which became reflected in the bark of the tree as if it were iron in the heat of a forge. The roots around Corvin rattled, then shot from out of the ground and encased his body in their searing tether.

The tree unbound at its foundation. Its shape morphed into concentric forms and contortions, hovering above the ruptured landscape. The roots and body of the tree contracted into a dynamic and ever-changing form, churning and lashing into a molten totem that left Corvin languishing in agony.

Uncountable moments passed while the stone-dust settled to the serenade of Corvin's helpless cries.

And then—like a clenched fist pummeling through desolated thatch-work—the tree recoiled, pulling Corvin into total darkness with a resounding clang that could shatter a thousand clouds.

§1B

Dazed and weary, Corvin felt as though he were falling for an eternity. The wrenching clatter of metal seemed to reverberate in the distant ground above, but the immediate surroundings were a black and sightless chasm.

Still fastened to the metallic lattice of branches, Corvin now felt as if he were dangling. The sensation of falling crept to a halt as whispers bounced into the void.

Buddha, Mother, Dagda, Shadow, Mantra, Nouma, Bloodlife, Eliš,
Buddha, Mother, Dagda, Shadow, Mantra, Nouma, Bloodlife, Eliš,
Buddha, Mother, Dagda, Shadow, Mantra, Nouma, Bloodlife, Eliš,
Buddha…

He could feel the shadow around him... pulsing, as if it were a thing. As if it had a heartbeat that was drumming with excitement.

Something between the sounds of a million trumpets and the infinite grating of metal poured into his ears and incredible wells of brightness beckoned like the arms of Zeus.

The points of light seemed kinetic in their motion, bundling until Corvin's vision was absolutely flooded with overwhelming blankness, where the line between the light and the void which came before it seemed to blur into enigma.

And then there was silence once more, manifesting only with the most gentle transience before Corvin found himself transported.

At first, it was the gentle call of the seagulls which beckoned him. The air and its motions contested warmth with a soft and tender playfulness, brushing the vulnerable skin of Corvin's chest, which was still very badly tarnished from the iron grasp of the tree.

The ocean's scent came to him as it rolled onto the shore, wresting his thoughts moment by moment with the bracing sublimity of its salt-sea brininess; and the sky was alight with a galaxy of stars that stained the heavens into the likeness of a gentle viridescent firmamence, reflecting a cornucopia of light and color on the water below; adorning the crest of its every wave and lapping.

Some ways away, a barefoot man wrapped in a tawny-colored robe stood next to a mound of books, which were haphazardly stacked behind him. Facing the sea, the sage seemed engaged in a continuous effort to cast these texts one-by-one into the beyond.

Corvin stepped forward, but then paused as his foot entangled one of the many errant documents which littered the beach between them.

"Stranger, stop what you are doing and tell me who I am speaking to," he said, approaching the figure with cautious steps.

The figure did not pause, but called out in reply, "Corvin Elrick Ratzinger. I had started to think you might never find your way down here."

The sage opened a leather-brown text with the word 'Phenomenology' stamped across the face of it. He tore out the back pages, leaving only a handful, then tossed the husk out into the ocean.

The clump of fitted pulp dangled between several fingers for a moment before falling to the sand underfoot. "I have a hundred thousand names, but you may call me El."

Corvin paused. "Alright, El it is."

"No," El replied. "It is not. 'It' is only called. And I, a humble servant, called to cast such aspersions against its Truth out to sea... If only they'd remain... vanished...What is it that you want of me?" the sage inquired, turning to face Corvin.

It was only then in the peering light that he noticed that the sage had no eyes. Dried and weathered bloodstains rested along the length of his cheeks while the sockets themselves were just empty.

Without blinking, Corvin answered. "I want to know why I'm here. I was brought here by a shadow who promised to help me fulfill my purpose, the deeper calling for which I was brought onto the Earth. Do you have the answer I seek?"

"When you give yourself to a task such as this, you find yourself forgetful of the rest." said El. "But I will show you your purpose, Corvin Elrick. Take my hand, and see as I see."

A vision captivated Corvin the moment his fingers touched the palm of El's hand. He felt as though he had been stitched into the fabric of world history: the enormity of his conscious gaze was of a god, and this state perplexed the very center of his being until his entire selfhood seemed dissolved, so that the ground of being was He, and he was the Ground of Being.

The voice of El shot out into the cosmic awareness, and in the stitching of the weave of Life, they sojourned with bold anticipation of the mystical.

"Once there was a being called Man. They were peculiar among the living in that every single one among them saw a whole world within itself. And so, when they came down from the trees and discovered the mysteries of fire, they believed that the power to name was wholly in their care. Through the rise of agriculture, the domestication of animals, and the mastery of tool-making, their languages claimed all that the light of their minds graced. But it was just the shadow of things, and when these clever beings had to die, it was all as dust."

"Longing for eternity, they reached ever-more-desperately towards that which remained before them—the names themselves, or else the act of naming. Twisting and contorting these languagings from their ordinary use, they contrived of ways in which they might preserve themselves through words alone."

"The pillars of civilization, religion, even science... all of it made from the labor of this yearning. And over time, each form of language became more rigid until they became sharp enough to cut against the soft creatureliness of Man. Words became enshrined as dogma. Enshrined as Eternal."

"But the Power of the Name was never theirs to wield. It was always Ours. We are the Eternal, they are our kin; younglings who have forgotten the ones who gave their Name—they, a world within each, are still but dust motes in the annals of time. Corvin..." said El with an air of finality, "remind them of what they have forgotten. Be Our harbinger, and claim for yourself the power of the Eternal."

Corvin pulled his hand away from El as if to save it from fire. He inhaled with a sharp desperation, as if expecting his lungs to be consumed with smoke and ash. But the air was clean.

"It is like this for everyone when they are first graced with the Light Eternal" said El.

Corvin breathed relief, "I'm not sure... what I am to do now."

El nodded. "When you awaken, you will find the world a very changed place. The society you know is one of kings, parliaments, and rule. Of politics and men. Humanity has since struck down these institutions, and replaced them with one on which the majority consents." explained El.

"Democracy?" said Corvin, "This was already unfolding in my time."

"Not the democracy you know, but yes." replied El. "It is a far more sophisticated thing, and radically conceived anew from the form of which you speak—the Ethocratic Republic, they call it. Yet at its heart still germinates its own demise in dark and twisted wanderings. With or without us, it will perish. At least let its death be a catalyst for Our return, a recollection of the right order of things."

Corvin nodded. "I understand."

El bowed his head with a potent solemnity. "Carry out your task, Corvin Elrick Ratzinger, and lay waste to the illusions which frustrate the happiness of all."

§IC

The howling wind of the icy caldera awakened Corvin, who was wrapped tightly in the trunk of the tree. The frost felt like a frozen flame against his arms and face, but nonetheless did Ratzinger smile. As he stepped forward, the wood which encased his body crumbled like ashes.

The wounds of the trial still left their mark upon his person, but when Corvin brushed the cusp of his shoulder and chest, the mark of it faded as if it had been drawn in pencil. The maul, once again in the clasp of his hand, now felt light as driftwood. In the distance, he saw a small figure cloaked in shadow. It was the shape of a snow leopard, and it sat perfectly still, meeting his gaze in the magic of the Dark.

"Creature!" Corvin exclaimed, "have you returned to me?"

"No, Corvin," the voice of the shadow called back, "I never left your side, though for centuries have you slept." And as quickly as the darkness had caught his attention, it dissolved into the night.

"Oh," said Corvin, "I just recognized your voice… El? Was it you all along?"

"Yes." said El. The night gripped Corvin, evaporating into his personhood as it spoke, "I am with you, being-in-the-flesh. Walk before me, and be thou perfect."

Corvin solemnly approached the rim of the Caldera, then slammed a mighty chasm into its facing with a swing of his hammer, beckoning the wake of his descent down the mountainside.

"Our recipe is simple yet indispensable to the palate of civilization—enough bread for all; not just for their own needs, not just so that they might break some with friends and loved ones freely—but also for abundant sharing with the other, the 'enemy', our neighbor. All of the Ethocracy is predicated on this ideal, and we exposit only on what must first occur in order for this to be accomplished."

— Edgar von Galen, *The Ethocracy*

§IIA

"Are Vanguards truly so fond of waiting, Ms. Anagonye?" Mr. Makgoba exhaled a silky cloud of breath—a bateful puff which tumbled gently into the dawning morn. Save for the muted sound of some or another vehicle passing distantly by—only the stiff gyrations of rain prevailed against the quiet air between them.

"The lecture concluded some time ago miss." said Mr. Makgoba, "Even you... can still catch a cold, I believe?"

Oni Anagonye stood just beyond the bus-length eaves of the Mandela Preparatory School for Gifted Children. Her kinky tresses of raven hair rustled in the cold wind, yet she stood undaunted, well-postured in the flight-suit of the Vanguard, which was streamlined with steel blue and shining grey synthetics.

Behind her was the young and honorable instructor Dawud Makgoba, whose well-manicured nails shined with far more prominence than his musty sable-stained shoes, fogged spectacles, and muted polyester bow tie.

"No." Oni muttered, breaking the silence.

"Oh, so you don't get sick anymore?" replied Dawud with a toothy grin.

"I'm not especially fond of waiting, to answer your question Mr. Makgoba," said Oni. "But the rain helps me think, so I don't mind... I appreciate your concern."

The heels of Mr. Makgoba's shoes tapped against the stone tiles beneath the alcove as he approached his former student. Dawud furnished a small umbrella from his back pocket, tossing its pastel fabrics skyward— purple, green, yellow, orange, and red twirling slowly as they rose. Oni grinned as the colors flashed across the gaze of her beaming hazel irides.

"I have missed having you in my class you know." said Dawud. "Though its been many years and you are now so accomplished in the academy, I'll never forget the eager young pupil you were when I first met you."

Oni smiled. "I've missed being there! It was an honor to observe you today, Mr. Makgoba."

"It's just Dawud now, friend," he gleamed. "Did I forget anything? In my lecture, that is. I'm somewhat rusty on the 18th century in Europe."

"Well..." Oni's stare wandered to a crevice in the walkway beneath them. "You misinformed your students at one point, but on the whole it was *really* an excellent presentation. I certainly wouldn't call you rusty by any means."

Mr. Makgoba shook his head. "Oh, I'm sorry to mislead them though. What did I get wrong?" After a momentary pause, Dawud traced Oni's gaze to the trickling rain at their feet.

"You referred to Kant as the 'father' of the Enlightenment, which is understandable... He's an important figure of it, to be sure. But he actually published his Critical works quite late into any historical consensus definition of the era."

"Oh, I uh," Mr. Makgoba stammered, " I must have heard it incorrectly when I studied at Cape Town. Teach me, friend."

Oni nodded. "Certainly, Mr. Makgoba." The faint smile on her face belied a modest tremor which had awoken in her hands and shoulders at that moment, though it did not show through her voice.

"I take it that you and I agree: the spirit of Enlightenment was namely in its intellectual optimism;" Oni began, "a strident Rationalism embodied in the notion that the power of human understanding would deliver us from many of the miseries, superstitions, and dogmatisms that characterized our past?"

Dawud nodded.

"Well," she continued, "if that's the case, and if we are particularly trying to get at the historical germination of the term, then I think it would be nearer the truth to suggest that Kant ended the Enlightenment than to call him its father."

"Really?" Dawud interjected with strong incredulity.

"Absolutely!" Oni affirmed. "After all, the Romanticists' aversion towards the unbridled intellectual supremacy of rationality was primarily seated in the profound relativism they perceived in Kant's *Critique of Pure Reason*."

A tirade of rain passed between them before Mr. Makgoba replied. "I see."

"Do you?" Oni said.

"No." Replied Dawud, "But I see I was mistaken."

The young Anagonye nodded her head reassuringly. "I hope you don't perceive this correction as an expression of any lack of trust in your abilities as an educator and scholar. You are amazing Dawud. Don't let some stuffy politician like me ever tell you otherwise."

Dawud reacted with an eager smile. "I appreciate that Oni. Thank you. The feedback is well-taken. I'll have to read up on it a bit more I think."

The gentle trotting of water on the broad-looped road of the school driveway served as soft recompense.

"Oni, I—oh." Dawud's voice trailed momentarily. "I just noticed— Your suit, it's..." Mr. Makgoba demurred.

Drops of rain streaked along soft crevices in the ground, seeding the beginnings of erosion. But as the specks came as if to dash against the cloth of Anagonye's suit, they stopped short. Blue light flickered ever-so-faintly an arm-span before it, and the rain could journey no farther.

"Yes, I know." Oni nodded, "It's quite strange. Better part of a year in and I still haven't adjusted to it completely. It's the armor's primary defense mechanism: any projectile which approaches us at a sufficiently threatening velocity is immediately vaporized. It may have saved my life a few times already..." said Oni, an eyebrow raised, pressing a finger against the breast of her suit as she spoke.

Her eyes wandered to the space above them, trailing the rain as it deflected off of Dawud's umbrella, and then back to her own more complex arrangement.

Somewhat sheepishly, though with an air of curious confidence, she continued, raising her hand as if to catch the mana as it fell, "apparently rain travels rather fast... Some would say it's a benefit, to keep dry in a storm."

Dawud tilted his head softly, "What do you think?"

Oni hunched her shoulder, "I think I'm quite fond of your umbrella."

Her former teacher laughed, "well is it something you can disable from time to time? I understand the great need to protect our Vanguards... but isn't this excessive? Save for some extremists who hide behind the anonymity of the Web, you are seen as heroes and scholars to us."

"I'm afraid the rules are not so amicable," Oni replied with a shrug, "but at least the precaution means that we cannot easily be attacked or debilitated. And it is important to remember: some of the more powerful Old World governments and corporations still have renegade actors who will do whatever they can to take power back."

"Ah yes. The Machiavellians." Dawud hummed. "I thought they were just an online scare tactic from those who don't accurately recall the cruelty of our former leadership... I suppose I was wrong."

Oni shook her head. "It's an unfortunate label: Machiavelli was a nuanced political theorist... more a Montaigne than a devil. The caricature is a functional portrait for politics in the Era of Subjugation though, I suppose."

Mr. Makgoba raised a finger with some exuberance. "AH! I read this as well, about Machiavelli! Benner's monograph, yes?" Oni nodded.

"Delightful. A classic, of course. You've always had excellent taste." said Mr. Makgoba, "Oni, the education you're receiving as a member of the Elect never ceases to amaze me... I am very proud, you know."

Oni Anagonye let out a soft, sweet murmur of a sigh, followed by gentle laughter. "Thank you Mr. Makgoba, but my favorite studies were when I was here, with you."

They stood in enjoyment of the rain for some moments.

"Be careful Oni," Mr. Makgoba remarked. "This suit... I don't think it is offered lightly. It sounds as though your duty has brought a target on your back."

"Yes," Oni replied, "that's the risk of public life. Though as you see, I am well-protected." She looked to her former instructor's eyes, which still held refuge beneath a furled brow. "But yes, Dawud, I promise I'll be careful."

"Thank you, Oni." he answered.

Yet another moment's silence passed.

"Oh and Oni, if I may?"

"Yes Dawud?"

"Please take a look behind you." instructed Mr. Makgoba. Dawud pointed up at the facing of the alcove, on which hung a wooden plaque with the words 'Nelson Mandela Preparatory School for Gifted Children' traced along the width of it.

"Do you know how far we've come, to have this?" said Dawud, "Do you know much we have had to overcome?"

Oni nodded.

"And did you know that Mr. Mandela believed that 'education is the most powerful weapon which we can use to change the world?' His words, not mine."

"Yes Mr. Makgoba."

"Well," Dawud began, "do you think this new government... the so-called 'Ethocratic Republic', aligns with that vision for our world?"

Oni shook her head, "No one anticipated von Galen's groundbreaking work, and as much as Mandela might have been happy with the best of it, I certainly don't think it's what he envisioned, per-se. But I do think he'd be pleased. It's a promising step for humankind."

Makgoba's eyes lit up against the cold day. "Perhaps... But it's all so fragile, isn't it? In these early years, somewhere in the back of our minds we are all still aware that it could be... otherwise."

Dawud paused for a few seconds until Oni nodded, after which he resumed. "It makes me think back to my senior seminar in undergrad, when we discussed the American Revolution and the years of its Early Republic: shortly after the war was over for the Americans, there was a radical curtailment of the promise of freedom, and the movement of the fledgeling nation was increasingly co-opted by wealthy interests."

"All of the bright idealism of the era of independence had faded to the harsh political realities of their life-world. It became so oppressive for our people in particular, even those as were free men and women, that my own ancestors were forced to flee to West Africa, to what would later become Liberia. Had the colonists genuinely intended for their vision of the 'shining city on a hill' to apply to everyone, I'd likely be an American."

"I see what you mean." Oni replied in a half whisper.

"What I'm trying to get at is both a caution and a worry." said Dawud, "My word of caution is this: if the Machiavellians really do have something that they can do to jeopardize or corrupt the spirit of the Ethocracy, history may be on their side. They do not have to militarily conquer our new government in order to ruin it. You must remain vigilant."

"I understand." Oni whispered.

Dawud lowered his head. "Do you?"

Oni lifted her shoulder, raising the strap of her knapsack on the crook of her arm. "I'll do my best Dawud. I appreciate your worry."

"That is not my worry." Dawud explained in a muted tone.

Oni raised an eyebrow, "What is it then?"

"My worry," replied Dawud, "is that this time, if there is a 'this time'... what is the next Liberia? What exodus is possible in a world where all countries are as one? If they come for our reclaimed wealth with fire and hatred, where do we go from there? All is entrusted in the success of the new order of things."

They stood rigid, the steady stream of time flowing ever onwards.

"As always, you've given me something to reflect on friend," Oni spoke, breaking the quiet. I still have much to learn from you, you know."

"And I you, Oni." Dawud replied with a grin, though in a moment it lessened. "I only wish your mother felt the same way... She stopped by the other day, you know, asking after you."

Oni bit her lip. "Oh, I- well, I suppose that's to be expected. I'm not sure what to say. It's just—" she began, but the words failed her. After a moment of discomfort, both of them tilted their heads sunwards, or where the sun presumably could have been seen on a clearer day. From the distance, a throttled hum began its descent from out of the cloudy skies above, expelling tonal bursts somewhere between the chirp of a morning dove and the gentle idling of a masterwork of motor engineering.

"It sounds as though your ride has arrived." Dawud called out against the pounding air. "Shall we say goodbye?"

"No not yet friend," Oni replied with a soft smile, "Tune into channel 78187 on your Porta-COM, I can speak for some time longer while in-flight if you'd like."

Her sleek conveyance was no larger than a sedan, descending on a 45 degree tilt. The top edges were styled with slender curves that came to a flat towards the back of the ship, while the bottom was dramatically cut, giving the ship a slender and agile appearance. Underneath the slicked wings were broad basins of yellow light, steadily fragmented by the mach-worthy motion of its bold steel-engine blades.

The ship itself matched the style of its owner's flight-suit: streaks of blue with grey accents across a polished, glossy hull. As it came to hover just above the ground, its nose tipped forward, and the glass plating of the cockpit came apart in five with the help of some steel-tube hydraulics; laying bare a body-formed seat and nothing more.

"Happily!" replied Mr. Makgoba, "I'll head over to my office and patch in now Oni. Catch you soon!" Dawud intoned with a wave of the hand, jogging off to the nearest side door of the Nelson Mandela Preparatory School for Gifted Children.

Oni leaned into the fitted shape of her ship's seating. Sturdy straps of fabric slid out from the corners of the crawlspace to secure her while the tempered glass came back to seal her in, and then in short order she vaulted far above the life-world of the school.

"Why 78187 if I may ask?" Dawud's voice peaked in over the com tech.

Oni laughed. "In reference to the publication dates of the first and second editions of Kant's Critique of Pure Reason, 1781 and 1787."

"You're joking." Dawud replied curtly.

"You short-changed my guy Dawud!" Oni answered, "Also, it's a palindrome. You know how I love palindromes."

The com went silent.

"Let me have my fun," Oni playfully pouted.

"Well alright then." Dawud sighed in resignation. "Have you named your ship yet?"

Oni droned a soft, uncertain tone. "Still thinking on that one. I want to make sure that the name matches the ship and the voice of my AI, you know? It'll probably be something that reminds me of home. Nostalgia is not useful for much, but it's really great for naming things, don't you think?"

"I suppose." replied Dawud. "Let me know what you come up with!"

The clouds bombarded the cockpit's plating with the subdued sounds of parted nature's tears. In time, the air grew dry and dim, while speckles of paintish light shined through the heavens to which Oni Anagonye ascended. The cracking of the Porta-COM sounded tinny, but clear.

"Oni?" called Mr. Makgoba, "Are you still there?"

"Sorry Dawud... I wish you could see this. It never ceases to take my breath away..." Oni thought for a moment, "the view, that is. The diminishing levels of oxygen, that does a bit. Take my breath away. When I say breath, You know what I'm—"

"Yes Oni, I know what you meant." Oni could hear Dawud's eye-roll. "Any chance you can share a video feed?"

"Certainly, though I really don't think it will be the same." Oni replied, toggling the Porta-COM's visuals. "We'll just have to get you up here sometime!"

"The view is perfect." said Dawud. "How amazing, Oni Anagonye... I am very happy for you."

"Aw, Dawud—thank you."

"I should be thanking *you* for this gift." he proclaimed. "Wow... it actually does feel like I'm seeing it with my own eyes. How is it so clear?"

"Well," said Oni, "my primary background isn't in science, but I believe the mechanism for Porta-COM technology involves leveraging the principle of quantum entanglement: particles spatially-separated, yet locked in a singular referential frame. A lot of our latest tech implements that principle from what I understand."

"I'll have to read up on it." Mr. Makgoba demurred. "It sounds like an important concept to know about."

A massive structure gradually came into view. Its body was entirely comprised of semi-translucent plating, and its various modular protrusions and extensions seemed to engage in gentle rotations independently of one another. Ten scores of vessels were attached to the hull throughout, and the faint glow of light from within the ship gave the Aeschylus an almost-golden luminescence.

"Hey friend, keep in touch." said Oni, "I'm about to dock. You'll call me if you need me, yes?"

"Always, Oni." spoke Dawud, "Take care."
The Porta-COM disengaged, and within moments Oni's ship grew close enough to illuminate a clear reflection of itself against the ship's facing. Yellow lights flared from each corner of the ship, which were then reciprocated by white ones along the Aeschylus.

Oni's vessel quickly aligned, and then pressed its face gently against the hull of the mothership. The panels gave way, and after a half-minute of compression, the glass cabin opened simultaneous with an opening in the hull, gently lifting Oni aboard.

§IIC

The room was sparse but aesthetic: all-white with light pouring out from dense, linear fretwork in the ceiling. Along the outer wall was a window bed overlooking the Earth. On the near wall beside a sliding door was a desk-surface which protruded from the wall.

"Computer, run rainforest simulation." said Oni. The lights dimmed, and all surfaces around her took the image of a tropical woodland in a gentle rain. The sound of thunder seemed to roll in the distance, and a warm, gentle mist quickly formed in the cabin.

"*Welcome home Oni.*" the computer offered with a luxurious croon. "*I'm glad to see you again. Can I offer you some home catering of your favorite herbal tea and a milk tart? Dining services are to begin at 18:00 local.*"

"That's okay computer," said Oni. "I can wait for my meal. For now I just want to relax. Thank you though."

"*I know you said that you want to relax,*" the AI replied, "*but Flight Officer Beckett is aware of your boarding status and is currently en-*

route to Sector K10. Ninety eight percent confidence, she will be seeking an audience with you. Should I decommission the simulation?"

"Yes. Oh, uhh- and alter protocol." Oni added, "when a superior officer approaches my quarters, inform me and end any simulations automatically."

"Code of Conduct: Aeschylus Protocol states that every member of the Vanguard is of equal social standing regardless of combat rank. You are not obligated to..."

Oni shook her head. "I know computer... Alright, maybe just make it for anyone who holds active member status." The simulation came to an end and the lights gradually re-engaged their standard function.

"Protocol altered." the computer confirmed. *"Your guest has arrived. Granting access."*

The sliding door parted from the wall, and Thea Mae Beckett stepped into the room. "It's good to see you Oni," Thea said. "I've missed you."

Oni smiled, "I've missed you too. Do you have a while to lie down? It's been a long day and I'd like to get a nap in before dinner."

Thea beamed, and the two of them lay down on the bed face-to-face. The lights dimmed after a few moments together.

"You know we're not going to get out of this bed until session begins." Thea whispered with a grin.

"Oh I know." Oni replied with a long, tender kiss on her lover's forehead. Parting, she rested her nose against the side of Thea's head, breathing in the rich aroma of sea fennel and lavender which had become so familiar to her over the previous months. "That's exactly what I want right now."

Oni rolled over, and with Thea's arm around her waist she touched the tips of her fingers to the plexiglass at the far end of the bed.

Gazing towards the starry skies beside her, she rested her arm on a threadbare copy of Edgar von Galen's *Ethocracy*, which lay flat against the windowsill. For once it would remain, and it was not long before Oni drifted into a deep and happy sleep—cradled in the arms of her sweet love.

"Make no mistake—the 'modern period' during the Era of Subjugation was intellectually no less of a dark age than Europe's early Medieval period. Their belief in the supremacy of personal opinion and whim was fomented by the ruling class, because a gentry who could not organize on principles of thought were pacified and made stupid, and thus were easy to overpower. They truly believed themselves to be the conquerors of history; that a tide of 'technology' and 'progress' would carry them to happiness, external forces over which they notably had absolutely no control."

"The real vehicle of power remains squarely in the universal inheritance of philosophy, but by convincing the masses that this was a fruitless pursuit, the wealthy conserved their domination—retaining this rich tradition for their own use in the gilded halls of the Academy —and in so doing pulling the greatest heist of all world history: convincing the peasantry that their precious gold was merely cheap, useless plastic. As the liberation fighter Assata Shakur taught us, 'No one is going to give you the education you need to overthrow them.'"

—Edgar von Galen, *The Ethocracy*

§IIIA

The steady reverberation of rubber treads rolled along ribbons of asphalt, which were propped up by the cement sequoias of a concrete jungle—an insignificant corner of the corporate district of Metropolis, the global economic capital formerly known as the city of Wien.

The bustle of urbanity signaled business-as-usual among the hustled traffic underneath the city's park-and-ride at Ravenna Boulevard. That morning as ever, citizens listlessly scuttled to acquiesce the labor of their fruit. The city ran like clockwork; sidewalk grates ticking with the predictable clacks of polished shoes from crowded passerby. A stroller rattled past: a new cog fitted to the old timepiece of a long and lost generation.

Dark as midnight, a pea coat flitted from out of the cover of a coffee stand at the bus station. Corvin straightened its collar along the crook of his neck. As he stepped into the stream of the working rank-and-file, its current flooded him with its dogging persistence and rigidity.

Shoulders checked, glares and sharp exhales deflected, eyes averted on the backwards stare: the pea coat saddled a holster occupied by a long steel piece. He straightened his waistband to conceal his weapon once more, leather gloves chaffing gently on the hilt. Sighing gently, he embraced the fleeting tenderness of the sound, gingerly breathing the aroma of the beverage in his grasp.

Corvin sat on a nearby bench, beside which stood a black and wiry post clock. And there he waited for some time, sipping the nectar of the Modern. The clock struck half past nine when he sat up, popped open the top of his coffee, and poured its remaining contents through the sewer grate before tossing it in the nearest receptacle. Corvin's breath rolled out as a warm cloud as he composed himself, condensing weightily through the air around him. It protruded for a moment with rich fullness before evaporating into the light of the cold grey morn.

He brushed past the pedestrian traffic with an erratic gate until he came to the entrance of a quaint shoppe, darting past its threshold unceremoniously. A sign hung tightly on the overhead of the establishment—a tawny slab of wood with the words *'Esquire Salon'* burned in bold, bright letters across it.

He pulled out a smoking pipe and well-worn plastic bag with long purple leaves inside it, wide and curled like crescent moons. Grabbing a handful, he crushed the dried herb in the palm of his hand and sifted its granules into the pipe's chamber.

After a few minutes of indulgence, Corvin began looking at his watch and peering inside—his foot tapping at the heel every half. Eventually, a client of the establishment pushed his way out the door, emerging into the assemblage of workers like a salmon in shallow waters. He tucked the pipe into his jacket and stepped inside briskly, hands in his pockets and shoulders pulled tight into his chest until he'd passed well into the interior of the stylish, modern salon.

A man with an empty gaze sat in a swivel chair affixed to the floor-space by a sink, his face covered in shaving cream. His gaze was directed aimlessly ahead. Corvin strode over to him quickly and turned about face, sitting in the chair next to the unshaved man with a dexterous kick in the air, tucking the higher leg above the other knee as his body came to rest on the pleather underneath him. The pipe reemerged, and Corvin let out a great cloud of smoke as he stretched his arms to the height of relaxation.

"Hey asshole," the adjacent client said, "No smoking in here." He pointed to the relevant signage, though Corvin did not acknowledge him. The unshaven man gestured to his stylist, who was across the room collecting razors. "Excuse me, could you—?"

The stylist nodded affirmingly before continuing to collect his gear. "Be right there!"

The client muttered under his breath. "Unbelievable. Seven years of loyalty and this is what I get? Preposterous."

"They can't see me you know." Corvin interjected, "Even if I permitted it, they wouldn't remember any of what's about to occur once I'm gone. As far as you need be concerned, it's just the two of us here. Or anywhere, for that matter."

The client's eye twitched. "Who are you? … you know what? Don't answer that, I don't care, and leave me alone. I'm not interested in any trouble."

Corvin turned his head to face the unshaved man. "Corvin Elrick Ratzinger. But that doesn't matter." he said. Tendrils of blue smoke unfurled from his nostrils like ivy, hanging in a trellis of thin air. Corvin grinned, "Actually, it's who you are that matters right now. And on that account, you ought to be *very* worried."

The client leaned into the far corner of his seat, his shoulders clamming inwards. "Well, Corvin," he replied, "I don't see any reason, I mean… Sir! Could you please?" he called with urgency, gesturing at the salonist, who quickly came to his side with tools in-hand and a raised eyebrow.

"Hey, sorry," the salonist said, "I didn't mean to keep you waiting. Shall we?"

The client balked, "No, we absolutely shall not, unless you can tell me a good reason why this lunatic hasn't been removed yet!"

A gunshot roared through the tight space between him and the stylist. The client stared in absolute and terrified disbelief as Corvin re-harnessed his piece calmly. Eyes wide as quarters and sinking ever further into the farthest edge of the chair, he yelled "Fucking Christ!"

The serving man spoke up sternly, "Sir, I'm not sure what you're on about, but if you cannot control yourself I will have to ask you to leave. Do we have an understanding?"

Corvin sighed, leaned forwards in his chair and turned to face the untrimmed man. "Yes Jeremy, do we? Oh, you are Jeremy aren't you? I'm sorry, this would be so embarrassing if I had the wrong person. I saw his name on the register on my way in and I just assumed from the photos..." Corvin trailed, fumbling through a small stack of polaroids from the lining breast pocket of his jacket.

The client began to sweat quite profusely and stammered incoherently. Vowels and consonants spilled out of his mouth, but the words they formed were scrambled far beyond the reach of intelligibility.

The salonist folded his arms, "I'm sorry but I can't serve you like this Jeremy. You'll have to leave." he said, offering a towel. Jeremy wiped his face, and he and Corvin stood in unison, the latter laughing heartily.

"Oh good," breathed Corvin, "I did get the right one after all. Oh Jeremy, don't try and run now. It's useless, really."

Jeremy booked it, dollops of shaving cream still smeared on his cheeks and chin. Corvin pulled the gun out of his holster once again and began his pursuit, shoving the entry door with his shoulder as he left.

§IIIC

The ground rumbled fiercely. Over the earth's roar, Ratzinger shouted, "there's nowhere to run Jeremy. Come and face me!" Jeremy sprinted past the traffic between them and the park-and-ride. Sharp breaths pounding out in the morning air were only halted when a truck, blaring its horn, slammed into his thigh and waist.

Jeremy fell onto the tar, his pant and shirt ripping across their seams. He picked himself up, looking over his shoulder. "Shit. I can't——" he muttered between bouts of strained wheezing. In the awkward pace between a limp and a jog, Jeremy faltered into the shadow of the highway above.

Corvin weaved seamlessly through the traffic, closing the distance between them with relative ease. "ENOUGH!" he bellowed, raising a lone gloved hand to the sky.

Great chasms ripped through the ground around the two of them. Traffic came to a screeching halt. The pillars of the overpass buckled and were torn. The highway collapsed, crumbling like a straw weave set afire. Concrete rain scattered dust and debris in an unbreathable shockwave.

The iron undergirding curled unnaturally with a serpentine writhing, breaking from their foundation and plunging into the ground around the two of them. The sound of it was like the unbridled scream of titans. Jeremy clenched his ears and fell limp onto the ground— huddled, weeping, and shaking uncontrollably.

34

Corvin closed the distance between them in slow, measured steps. He crouched, pulling the slide of his semiautomatic as he brought his face towards the ground tilted, meeting Jeremy's contorted gaze. The commotion settled, and a gust cleared the debris around them. Yet the concrete haze persisted in the distance, a curtain between them and the world. Once the dust had settled, Corvin broke the silence. "Tell me Jeremy, does the name Ashley Lanning mean anything to you?"

Jeremy shook his head. Corvin jolted, thrusting the barrel of his gun into Jeremy's temple with such force that his head slammed into the ground. "Don't. Fucking. Lie. One more chance Jeremy. Tell the truth."

Jeremy, hyperventilating, mustered a response. "Y-yes okay, yeah I know her, of course I know her, we were together for years. Please."

Ratzinger let up for a moment. "Then you know why I'm here."

"N-no not really." Jeremy stammered." I mean, what, did she send you here?"

A moment of silence passed. Corvin stared into Jeremy's eyes with somber connotation. "No." he said flatly. "She can't send anyone anywhere. She's in the hospital. Bloody. Unconscious... They said she won't likely live much longer."

Jeremy sat up, brow furled as he shook his head in a tight, frantic motion. "No no no no that wasn't me. I didn't do that, no I haven't seen her in weeks. Please, this is a misunderstanding."

Corvin sat up to a kneeling position, resting the gun on the peak of his raised leg. "Oh Jeremy, you did do it to her though. That, and so much more, didn't you? Don't shake your head like that, I'm sure you know exactly why she's there."

Jeremy's shudders parted a long breath before he answered. " I mean, yeah... I think so. Did she do it again? Try to kill herself?" Corvin nodded, "well," He continued. "that's not me. She's been suicidal for well over a year. Ever since her mother. I did what I could."

Corvin grabbed Jeremy's jaw. "Did what you could? You drank, broke her treasured things in a pathetic attempt to assert dominance. You belittled everything she did. Pressured her. You beat her. I don't know if you knew she was pregnant. I don't care. You took her child from her. She had decided to keep it, that's why she tried to get you to stop drinking, to stop *with* her, the night you... sick fuck."

Save for the gust passing by, all was deafening silence. "Do you know she can't feel anything in that hand now? Do you know, she kept her bangs over her face, to try and hide what you'd done."

"Her beautiful face, hidden from the world. You took her confidence. You took her smile... You took her happiness, and now she decided to take her life. Own it." Ratzinger drew his thumb along the top of the hammer of his pistol.

Click.

Jeremy stood up, slowly dusting off a caked film of cement on his person. He wiped his nose and breathed in sharply. Blood was smeared on his mouth and cheek. His prolonged exhale lowered the tempo of his panic momentarily. "You're going to kill me here, aren't you? I'm going to die here." He let out a gentle sob.

"Yes," Corvin hissed. "You took my daughter from me. You are going to die in a moment, Jeremy Everett Langdon. But before I take your life, I need you to understand something."

Jeremy heaved a trembling cry and took a few moments of weathered gasps before speaking any more, "I understand. Actually, I do. I don't want to—please, but, yes, I know why I just—please Corvin. I'm scared. I don't want to die. I'll be better, I'll do better, just don't do it. You're better than this, better than me. You don't have to kill me!"

Ratzinger slowly shook his head. "You misunderstand Jeremy. You think I came as a harbinger of justice. No." Corvin stepped forward. "I come to murder you. Why do you think I didn't just crush you with these pillars? With powers like these," Ratzinger gestured to the scene around them, "why do you think I brought a gun? There were a hundred different ways I could have taken your life by now, or permanently detained or disabled you, if all I wanted was to stop your cruelty in this world."

Jeremy sat there, shaking without a word. Ratzinger leaned inwards, cradling the back of his neck. He raised the gun to Jeremy's temple; polished steel muddied with sweat, blood, and dust. Ratzinger spoke softly, "You killed my daughter Jeremy. Now look into my eyes. Tell me what you see."

Corvin's iris was like a scratched and shattered mirror. In its reflection, all of the chaos and wreckage of the scene around them played out like film, the details of which were muddled by the eye's many folds and imperfections. The highways collapsing, the pillars snapping like evergreens struck by lightning, the undergirding. All of it.

And suddenly, Ratzinger's eye morphed once more. The iris became clear like a silver basin, and Jeremy saw himself and Ratzinger with perfect clarity, standing together just as they are now with the traffic of the day's business right behind them. In the vision, Corvin pulled the trigger and Jeremy saw his own body crumpling to the ground, lifeless.

"I see." Jeremy whispered.

Corvin nodded. "Yes. I imagine you do."

A shadow emerged from out of Corvin's jacket, looming far across the park-and-ride at Ravenna boulevard. It was marked with black and jagged contours, but its body was smooth and refined like silk, and was stretched along the street in the shape of feathered wings.

"Just do it Corvin, for Christ's sake." the voice of El rasped from behind him.

Corvin's hand slipped from the cusp of Jeremy's neck upwards, reaching to encompass the base of his skull with a narrow and menacing grasp.

"This mind." Ratzinger growled, "It took my daughter away. Abused her, erased her identity, and tormented her. Neurons and synapses, networked and firing like lightning cast through the storm clouds of a summer valley; cascading these horrible ideas and intentions through the little universe... the ideas and expressions of which constitute what we call—you... Well—"

Corvin retracted his arms quickly, slamming his palms against his victim's chest, hard as a piston. Jeremy stumbled backwards. As he sat up, struggling for breath, Corvin wheeled around and lifted the barrel of his pistol. With a muted but emphatic tone, he called out, "I deny your universe, Jeremy Langdon."

The bullet clanged like thunder through the wreckage of Metropolis. Once the sound settled, the calamity was no more: the pillars and highways restored, and the busybodies walking past as if nothing whatsoever had occurred.

Corvin took three sharp and segmented gasps, retching towards the dusty, well-worn tar of Ravenna Boulevard. His breathing slowed, and then with quiet solemnity he rose.

The shadow floated to fill the space behind him. "Why the performance? We only needed him for his clearance to the National Archives as an accredited Bibliographer. I mean kill the boy, by all means, but—What was the point of all this? It's not as though the girl was really Our daughter."

Corvin rose, "They are each and every one Our children, El. We are All-Father, and we have come."

"Justice is what love looks like in public, just as tenderness is what love looks like in private."

— Cornel West, *Sermon at Howard University*

Chapter Four

§IVA

The light of Thea's personal quarters was a soft, dim amber. Each wall mimicked the fine paper of a painted byōbu partition, and the music was a warm and delicate biwa melody that honored the cherry blossom —some of which was intermittently projected holographically into the space of the cabin.

Oni and Thea were joined by the other two members of of their unit, K10 Theta. The first, Corporal Leveigh Simoneau, was a dour-faced young man in an unbuttoned flannel shirt; the sleeves of which were rolled just before the elbows. His hair was a long clutter of mouse-brown threads, and although his expression was sharp, he carried himself with a serene and gentle disposition.

By contrast, Corporal Michael Kuhn held himself with a subdued energy that belied his hectic and frenetic mind. He wore a plain long-sleeve shirt the color of English custard. Jasmine tea sat in the palm of his hands, and ragged flip-flop slippers hung off the lengths of his feet, which looked almost as comfortable as they were impractical.

"So," Michael wondered while wafting the floral vapors of his teacup, "you guys ready for the mission tonight?"

Leveigh frowned. "To be honest… I'm still not clear on why we're just sitting here waiting." he admitted testily. "Shouldn't a kidnapped Senator be filed under 'urgent situation requiring immediate attention'?"

Oni sat up to reply. "It's a security thing," she explained. "Here, take a look at the layout." She gestured to the wall, which opened up a regional topography of the location. The label 'Balata-Tufari national forest, Brasil' was kerneled tight under the bottom right corner of the projection.

"You see that encampment over here?" she offered, pointing to the map.

Thea took over, "Their line of sight is made vulnerable over the run of the river when the Sun hangs over the tree-line in the evening."

Oni nodded. "If we come in from relative West during that time, we minimize the risk that they execute Senator McKinley before we can neutralize the guards on him. We believe they mean to use him as a bargaining chip for removing our blockade in Panama, so they'd be unlikely to take his life unless they think they've lost control of the situation. Still, the Regulatory Committee aboard the Prometheus wants us to take every precaution, and of course High Command is happy to oblige."

Leveigh laughed in disbelief. "But like, we have super-soldier invincibility suits and can travel as fast as a jet while still the size of tiny people. This isn't caution, it's paranoia. Caution is sending a single Vanguard literally whenever instead of your ordinary platoon of local security forces. One look at our magic armor and anyone who still has dry pants is probably already on the ground with their hands behind their heads." The room was weighted evenly between laughter and raised eyebrows.

"That kind of magical thinking is going to get you in real trouble someday." said Thea, "Don't look at me when you get your ass blown out."

Corporal Simoneau grinned. "You spend a lot of time thinking about my ass there officer?"

Thea's brow flew high as she grabbed a pillow from the bed, throwing it at him. "Not at all: they'll think they're aiming at your face." she zinged. Leveigh play-bowed in a bemused state of abjection and effacement.

Oni, who had been pinching her chin throughout this banter, spoke up with a smirk. "He's right though, love. It is ridiculous. Of course the magic armor will suffice. Also, fairies are real, and the good sir Leveigh is destined to save princess-senator McKinley in a properly stalwart fashion before being knighted by our great king Aeschylus, long may he live. How dare us knaves stand in the way of his glory!"

Michael wagged his finger. "Now don't you go giving our whimsical friend any ideas… I'm not entirely convinced that he doesn't actually believe in magic."

Leveigh squinted, sucking down a shot of rice wine in a spurt of self-caricature. "I mean what's the difference though?" he began, "Either way we are completely invincible to them and wield power beyond their wildest imagination. Call it magic, call it technology… at the end of the day it's all the same really, isn't it?"

Thea and Oni's eyes opened wide, the latter half-whispering, "Oh he did not just go there in front of Michael…"

Thea shrugged. "There goes our afternoon."

Corporal Kuhn cleared his throat. "As the only Vanguard here with an advanced degree in the natural sciences, let's just get one thing clear—it's really, really not the same; and, you can be confident in that because you didn't die at nine and a half years from polio, nor were you put to fire on suspicion of witchcraft the moment some sexually-frustrated patriarch caught you with a copy of *Philosophical Investigations*."

Thea hesitated. "So you've never seen anything science can't explain? I'm of course not saying I think magic is real, but—"

"I mean never say never," Michael interjected, cutting Thea off, "of course there are things science hasn't been able to explain, and may never be able to. That doesn't exactly make us wizards though, does it... Oni, you have any fresh ideas you'd like to inject into this conversation?"

They all turned to face Oni, who sat with her arms wrapped around bunched legs, her top lip pressed contemplatively between pointer fingers. "I'm with them, Michael. Sorry."

Michael's jaw dropped in disbelief. "Are you serious? That's crazy. You actually have some background in the sciences too... Okay, explain your reasoning. Please."

Oni took a deep breath. "I imagine that somewhere on one of the million-million planets that we currently speculate could support life—"

"Try forty billion," Michael interrupted once more.

"No, you're about four years out-of-date on the literature with that figure." Oni explained, "Lots of work on non-carbon-based life has shown that estimate to be laughably conservative. May I continue?"

Michael nodded. "Sorry," he said.

"Thanks," Oni replied. Corporal Kuhn winced at Oni, who grinned briefly before regaining her thought-process. "Anyways, on one of these planets—there probably exists a species which naturally adapted the capacity for propulsion-based flight instead of relying on wing-caused lift like in life on earth."

"Now, if they were to come to Earth and could survive our atmosphere, imagine the stares they would get for doing what is as natural to them as breathing is for us. But then we would study them, and implement the insights their biology could teach us into our own material culture, and then this capacity of theirs would be matter-of-course for us."

Michael fidgeted before responding, "... I don't take your point. We developed that tech without this hypothetical being; it's central to the utility of our flight-suits. This is superfluous, and wildly speculative."

Oni laughed. "Of course it's speculative! Your query is grammatical, not theoretical. You're asking about the value of understanding 'magic' and technology in-conjunction. That's just about our use of words, and has nothing to do with the existence of things at all, so thought experiments are really the only way we have to test the use-cases of a notion."

"But I suppose this example might be too much of an abstraction. Let's not get caught up in murky waters. How about something more concrete?"

Michael nodded, upon which Oni resumed. "Suppose we go down there for our mission tonight and the insurgents are equipped with their own radically-advanced technology that we don't understand. What feelings would it instill in you?"

Michael demurred. "I don't know... I guess if it significantly out-stripped the capacity of Vanguard technology, my response would be terror, obviously."

Oni continued, "and what's the difference between that and the creature I mentioned earlier?"

"Well," replied Michael, "the creature isn't intent on killing me."

Oni shook her head. "Ontically, Michael. I mean to ask—what's happening differently for them in terms of their capacities?"

Now it was Thea who interjected. "The Machiavellians are creating the capacity for themselves, whereas the creature had it merely as a fact of its birth. That's what you're getting at, right Oni?"

"So what," began Michael, catching Oni's nod to Officer Beckett, "all technology is just prosthesis for survival functions, and the difference between magic and whatever level of functioning a person has just boils down to our understanding of it and the power-relationship that creates?"

His compatriots, exchanged glances before affirming one another.

Corporal Kuhn squinted, pinching the nave of his nostrils. "No, what? Guys, we are talking about existence here. Does magic exist? No. Does technology exist? Obviously."

Oni whipped out her reply, ready-made. "No, not obviously. As an idea, 'technology' has no referential substance which might beg a name attached to a particular. It's a social phenomenon, just like magic: it's one way we speak about the important happenings around us. Before the advent of modernity, we were scared and mystified by the world in which we found ourselves. The thought of 'magic' gave agency to the lived uncertainty of life; it codified a unity to any strange otherness which a community felt ought to be called dangerous."

"Technology… it's just a way of centering our narrative on human intelligence and ingenuity as a way of confronting any maligned 'otherness' while exploring a world of possibilities. It's a potent notion… but our desire to valorize its potency as if it had some moral force… it blinds us to the ways in which really, all we're talking about is the augmentation of human potential to answer possible threats. The magic is in *our* hands now, and so what was once wondrous has now become practical."

"But that power—it is engaged in our sins just as much as in our triumphs. Think of Auschwitz and Dachau, Hiroshima and Nagasaki, Vietnam, Syria and Yemen. Think of Washington and Moscow. When we reflect on all the misery technology is capable of amplifying… how can we not find ourselves caught up in the same mystified terror of our ancestors?"

"There is a stupefying force in ourselves which we can scarcely understand, and whether in ourselves or in the world—technology has pushed us to the limits of what is possible of our species. We may find ourselves in need of a word like 'magic' again sooner rather than later, my friend."

Michael shifted his weight for a few seconds before meeting Oni's gaze. "Consider me a skeptic." he said, with a warm-yet-reserved shrug.

Oni's eyebrow raised along a smile. "That is reasonable. All of what has been said here is reasonable." She shimmied over to Michael and put her arm around his shoulder, "Don't let your brain get too mushed though: we've got quite an evening ahead of us."

Michael gently huffed, running his hand through his hair. "Hey Leveigh, you got any more of that sakē?"

Leveigh tossed the bottle to his friend across the aisle.

"2500 meters." Oni said through the Porta-COM tech as K10 Theta stood along the belly of their transport ship.

Thea pulled a lever, opening access from the hull into the open air. "We can't risk getting any closer by ship. They might notice our approach. Get going Vanguards." And with that, the four of them pirouetted out of the transport and into the heavy haze of the Amazon.

The encampment gradually shifted into sight as they cut through the evening light like blackbirds, sleek and dark blots gliding along a bold and radiant horizon.

Michael spoke up. "It looks like the prisoners quarters aren't heavily guarded. I should be able to make quick work of the insurgents there and make sure no civilians are hurt."

"Good," said Thea. "Oni and I have the Senator. If our intel is right, he's in that structure at the corner of the encampment. Leveigh you ready—"

Leveigh gave a thumbs up. "Alright K10 Theta. Let's get this party going." He rocketed swiftly to the center of the camp. "Computer, you know the one. Hit it." Just as he said those words, a classic rock song belted out with deafening loudness. Kicking up a wave of dirt as he landed, Leveigh began air-guitar rocking just before the bullets started flying.

"Isolate the frequency K10 Theta." ordered Thea. After complying, they went to their respective positions, the ballad drowned out from their COM tech.

Several armored cars pulled forward to the prisoner's quarters. As the men started filing out, Corporal Kuhn shot two needle-sized missiles from his wrists into the back end of the vehicles. "Computer, neutralize." said Michael, followed by dark billowing smoke from each car's engine.

Landing, Corporal Kuhn grabbed one Machiavellian insurgent by the arm, whipping him around to slam two others horizontal like bowling pins. Several other soldiers filtered forward, but when Michael lifted his hand warningly, they stopped in their tracks and lowered their weapons. "Smart choice." he replied.

"Now who has the keys for the prisoners? Or do I just need to breach the locks myself? Hello?" The insurgents who had laid down arms were covering their ears, protecting themselves from the deafening melodic effusions of Leveigh's flight-suit.

As Michael worked to open the digital locks on the cell doors, several of the Machiavellian insurgents who had been firing at Leveigh turned their guns at the prisoners. Leveigh, who was keeping his eyes further afield to look out for activity towards the Senator's holding station, remained oblivious. As the prisoners sunk back in their cells, Michael turned to see several assault rifles pointed at his wards.

He rocketed forward, firing mechanical bolas from his hand to bind up most of them as he closed the gap on the remaining two. Grabbing the rifle from out of the first one's hands, he cleaved the man down with a measured thwap on the chest. Michael Jetted over to the second Machiavellian just in-time to catch the combatant's bullet through his hand, stemming its velocity.

Corporal Kuhn bent the barrel of the gun before the next shot was taken. It backfired, blowing back sparks which burnt the hand of its owner. "Congratulations," Michael grunted, "you're one of the elite few who have actually managed to wound a Vanguard." He slammed his injured fist into the Machiavellian's nose, who collapsed like a stack of cards. "History will smile upon you fondly, I'm sure."

As the gunman crumpled to the ground, Michael looked at the hole through his hand, which trembled from pain. "Computer, is my wound reparable?"

The AI replied, "*Yes Corporal, but it will hurt, even with the local anesthesia I applied at the moment of injury. Should I begin the operation?*"

Michael shook his head. "Not yet, just treat it for now. I'll have medical look at it when we get back."

"*Understood.*" the computer responded, filling the gap with a rigid foam. The rest of the Machiavellians having either fled or surrendered, Corporal Kuhn sat in a nearby empty chair by a makeshift fire pit.

Leveigh ran forward.

"Hey, you okay?" he called.

Michael nodded. "Yeah, just a scratch." He laughed, still shaking. "I wasn't thinking right and I let that guy breach my shield-space with his gun. Might as well just have walked my hand right into a knife."

Leveigh brushed off the comment. "Nah, not the same. In the heat of the moment, sometimes instinct takes over. Lots of evolutionary impulses to overcome to use this tech effectively. You slipped up. It happens. You're the one who taught us that when we were newbies, remember?"

Michael laughed as Oni and Thea walked out, a weak and battered older man supported in their arms. He and Leveigh stood up, jogging towards them.

"Senator McKinley!" Leveigh called.

The senator looked up, and nodded meekly. "Thank you for coming to get me, K10 Theta. I was beginning to think that maybe I would never be a free man again." The shuttle came into view, and the lot of them boarded, stowing the senator safely on-ship. Thea fired a flare into the sky above the encampment, and then they were space-ward bound.

"Senator," said Oni softly, "we know you've been through a lot. From the looks of it, you've been beaten pretty badly, and you seem sleep-deprived. Rest up. We'll get you and Corporal Kuhn to medical aboard the Aeschylus and then someone will be with you to debrief you and make arrangements for a comfortable re-entry to public service."

---

§IVC

Once again, K10 Theta sat in Thea's private quarters. This time, the projection was a canoe upon the wide-open delta of a temperate river. In the distance, blue mountains hugged with snow intricate as lace rounded the vista while bright green coniferous trees swayed gently in the wind. Oni and Michael had beers, whereas Leveigh and Thea drank blackberry and raspberry lemonades, respectively.

"Something doesn't feel right." Michael said flatly.

Leveigh nodded his head in a parody of earnest concern. "Yes... I don't want to unsettle anyone, but... I think we may be in some sort of simulation."

Michael was not amused. "I just looked at the debriefing report from the senator. He officially claims that he had been kept in holding between interrogation sessions."

"And?" said Thea.

"That's a lie." Michael explained. "I saw the logs for the jail cells myself. No one had been transferred in or out for three days; which is longer than the time Senator McKinley was on-sight."

"Michael," Thea responded, annoyed, "he was badly concussed and hadn't slept in days. He was probably just delirious. Memory handles duress poorly."

Corporal Kuhn pursed his lips. "Yeah… you're probably right." The lines on his expression eased. "You know Oni, I've been giving some thought to what you said earlier, about the line between magic and technology… I think I'm starting to see what you mean."

Oni's eyebrow raised. "Yeah?" she said, curious.

Michael nodded. "Yeah, it got me thinking about the 20th century chemist George de Hevesy. When the Nazis came to occupy Denmark, Hevesy feared that his colleagues Max von Laue and James Fanck would have their Nobel Prize medals stolen."

"So he dissolved the gold medallions in aqua regia, knowing that he could reverse the process if ever the Nazis were defeated, and that in the meantime they would be passed over as some valueless solvent. And it worked: the Nobel society re-minted the awards at the fall of the Third Reich, and presented them to Franck and Laue once more."

Thea's brow firmed up. Nodding, Michael continued. "Aqua regia. King's water. Dragon's blood. It's a substance discovered by Europe's alchemists in the 14th century. Its properties wouldn't be described in the scientific literature for another half-millennia… It really is about the language we use Oni. I take your point."

Leveigh opened his eyes wide, running his fingers along the projection on the floor. "Guys, the water… it's just linoleum tiling. Our whole life is a lie!"

"Hey bonehead," Thea laughed, "that's not linoleum."

Leveigh threw a pillow at his friend across the bow. "Oni, permission to keelhaul your lover for insubordination?"

Oni nodded, Thea gasped, and Michael grinned as the shenanigans deepened; yet despite their ensuing play and struggle, the boat never rocked.

"Authentic political leadership participates in and lifts up all the vital workings of society. Therefore, the ethical state requires more than someone who will merely make decisions for the public: if they cannot be teachers, mentors, and vanguards of the peace… they are not worthy of our endorsement. And still, this only earns our admiration: for if we are to entrust something as precious as the future of our species to an individual, they must also be deeply learned to claim stake in our confidence—knowing what they do not know, observing with the keen sight of genius the finitude of their own understanding."

— Edgar von Galen, *The Ethocracy*

Chapter Five

Oni sat up from the bed, where Thea Mae Beckett lay resting. She brushed her eyes, then sat still. The room lay silent and dim in a quiet for which only a gentle sigh could be mustered. "Computer," Oni whispered, "run back yesterday's presentation through Porta-COM visuals. Set audio to private."

"*Running simulation.*" the Computer replied "*Video analysis suggests non-lyrical music at .36 standard volume would not be intrusive to your comprehension based on past performance. Should I play something for you?*"

"New-wave Lofi fusion with rich tonal characteristics please" said Oni. The beat swelled, the lights dimmed, and the hologram projection was cast into the living space of her quarters.

The scene was the classroom at the Nelson Mandela Preparatory School for Gifted Children. Dawud leaned on the desk behind him, aside which was Oni, arms nested across her chest. The kids, mostly freshmen, were quiet and attentive as Dawud spoke.

"And, that's probably it for today," he said, looking at his watch. "Because—... I want to take some time to introduce you to a very special guest. This young woman beside me," Dawud pointed, "her name is Oni Anagonye. Believe it or not, she is one of the Elect aboard the Aeschylus. How did we get a member of the Elect, a Vanguard no less, to visit us? Well, I'll let Ms. Anagonye explain that to you. Please welcome our guest!"

Dawud stepped aside as Oni came to the front of the class. The students clapped respectfully.

"Hey there!" Oni said somewhat sheepishly. "It's great to be here and come visit you. Mr. Makgoba introduced me well, so I'll get right to the point."

"The reason I'm here today is to support your education, which is vital to maintaining the health and activity of your government. This month, thousands of Vanguards and Senators are touring schools across the planet as part of our oath of office to promote the vitality of our democracy."

A small boy in the back of the room raised his hand. "Yes?" Oni called.

The boy lowered his arm. "Pardon me ma'am, but I know that not all of my classmates have a firm concept of how our planetary government works. Could you give a brief overview of what Senators and Vanguards do?"

Oni nodded. "Absolutely! What's your name young man?"

"Cameron miss." he said.

"Thank you Cameron! So, we have a bicameral system of government divided into the National Academy aboard the Prometheus and the Chamber of Discourse aboard the Aeschylus. These institutions were put into space at the founding of our government as a compromise between nations. When the Ethocracy was founded fifteen years ago, the vast majority of nation-states ratified its constitution. Nonetheless, the territorial anxiety of their warring and fragmented pasts prevailed when deciding on the location of the houses of power."

"It was proposed that since the nexus of research and legislation would reach a singularity in this new government anyways, it would be advantageous to all for us to house these institutions in the territory-neutral and research-rich environment of space, housing represent-atives from across the planet. On the ground, for those who live or are operating on the surface, Capitol buildings were established in the former offices of power in the old Wien quarter in Metropolis, or Vienna, as some of the West knows it."

"Now I know I'm giving you a lot of information so I'm going to hone down really specifically to what I think prompted this question, which was your natural curiosity about Senators and Vanguards. Senators, operating from out of the Prometheus, are responsible for crafting and ratifying our laws. They are not only trained experts in the process for doing so, but also hold PhDs from accredited universities in any subject on which they wish to write legislation."

"Within the National Academy, there are two rounds of voting. The first is closed, meaning that the vote is only among others who have at least some significant university background on the subject at hand. Usually a minimum of a bachelor's degree is required to partake. Essentially, this means that only environmentalists vote on matters of the environment, healthcare experts vote on healthcare, economists on taxation and the budget, et. cetera."

"This requires a two-thirds supermajority to pass into open voting, where the whole Academy gives its verdict. A bill which has passed closed voting only requires a simple 50% majority of senators to move to the Chamber. The vast majority of these bills which pass closed voting make it to the chamber. There are also committees on economics, logistics, and security that closed-vote counsels often consult when crafting their legislation. These committees require a PhD as well. Does all of this make sense so far?"

There were several nods across the classroom as Cameron replied, "I think so. But what do Vanguards do?"

Oni beamed, "I'm glad you asked. We Vanguards have a more… abstract role. Our PhDs are all squarely in moral philosophy and ethics, though many of us hold advanced degrees in other fields. We don't craft our own legislation, but instead audit the output of the National Academy. Once a bill has a two-thirds majority from the members of the Aeschylus, it becomes law."

"So," said Cameron, "why is it called the 'Chamber of Discourse' then?"

"Good question," Oni replied, "So, as I mentioned, Vanguards don't have nearly as much legislative work as Senators. It's like the ethics panel of a hospital: doctors have other responsibilities, right?"

Cameron nodded.

"Well," said Oni, "Since Vanguards are charged with the monumental task of representing the conscience of the people… a lot of our spare time is dedicated to self-imposed seminars where we discuss pressing issues in society, topics in philosophy, et. cetera. Hence the name. A lot of what happens there is the cross-pollination of ideas—kind of like with professors at a university, but where they are also the students."

A girl in the front of the room nearest the door raised her hand. Oni pointed, and she spoke, "but Ms. Anagonye, how can they speak about pressing issues in society if they don't live in it?"

Oni's grin spread from cheek to cheek. "Wonderful. An excellent observation. What is your name young lady?"

The girl touched her cheek. "I'm Aiyana, but my friends call me Aiya. You can call me Aiya, miss."

"Haha, okay thank you Aiya," said Oni, "So, Vanguards had a huge conference when the Aeschylus was first built called the Conference of Nations, and that was one of the three major issues on which the conference focused. Another was the topic of law enforcement and the problem of state violence. We answered both those problems together. Vanguards are charged with the protection of the people."

"This suit I'm wearing... in many ways, it gives me powers like a superhero. You've all read comic books and watched the old hero movies, right?" said Oni. Most students nodded.

"Great! I'm a big fan too. But yeah, it's somewhat like that: the suit gives us greatly heightened strength and agility, short-range flight capabilities, near-invulnerability. We train to make the best use of these enhancements. We are in touch with community peace-keeping initiatives all across the planet, and as soon as we're called, we dispatch a team to handle any volatile situations which exceed the capacities of our ordinary responders."

"Because of the advantages afforded us with our technology, the world-class training we receive, and the amazing support given from these community activists, the fatality and injury rates are extremely low; both for the community watchdogs themselves and for those who breach the order of the peace."

"We also pledge 160 hours of community service a year, focusing on civic and social leadership initiatives from every walk of life. Does this answer your question Aiya?"

The girl nodded with a smile.

"Alright class," Dawud interjected, "looks like it's time for lunch. Thank you Oni for coming to speak with us today. See you kiddos in the afternoon."

The children stood up to leave for lunch, but before they exited the room, Oni called out, "Oh, Cameron and Aiya, can I speak with you two for a second?" The two children came to the front of the class.

"Hey," said Oni, "It was really great to hear from you two in class today. You are smart, thoughtful young people. The Ethocracy will be better off for having you among it. So I just wanted to thank you." She smiled.

Cameron beamed back at the Vanguard, and Aiya replied, "thank you miss." And with that, the two young children followed after their classmates.

§VB

The hologram faded.

Thea rolled over, eyes gently rising open as she gazed up at Oni. "Hey love," she said, "what's up? Are those tears?"

"Yeah." Oni nodded.

"You okay? What's wrong?" asked Thea.

"I don't know. I'll be fine, no worries." said Oni, wiping away the gentle stain on her cheek aside a dim smile.

"Okay," her partner replied tenderly. "Well, you let me know if I can help... I—"

The lights aboard the Aeschylus went out in a wave of sweeping uniformity, crashing against the blackness of beyond. The darkness flipped into a pale blue, and with it went all warmth in the room as a voice came on the intercom.

"This is an official announcement from the General Assembly of High Command aboard the Aeschylus. Code blue. All active personnel, please report to Amphitheaters A, C and D for briefing on an urgent matter concerning global security. Again, this is code blue. This message is not a drill and your presence is required. Thank you."

By the time Oni and Thea had made it down to the fourth Amphitheater, crowds of Vanguards in the hundreds were already filtering their way through the entrance in rapid succession.

Once they were settled, a hologram of a face with ambiguous features emerged from out of the floor-work of the staging at the head of the theater. It spoke with the voice of the ship's native intelligence, giving a report of the circumstances in a metered and efficient style.

"Hello everyone, thank you for your attention. Reports from the ground indicate that at 06:00 hours, that is, 15 minutes ago aboard this ship, a heavy contingent of Machiavellian insurgents stormed the Federal district of Metropolis. First vanguard response, seventeen in number, have reported an initial estimate of around four hundred combatants."

"Among those who have been positively identified by our first responders are several members of the notorious Machiavellian Strike Force known as 'The Ravenous Four', which is the only known unit to have ever caused lethal Vanguard casualty. Be advised not to engage insurgents with a raven crest or insignia unless explicitly ordered to do so in your briefing, which will commence en-route to Metropolis."

"Some of the enemy come from outside the perimeter of the Federal district and have successfully overwhelmed our ground security forces. Others appear to have been deep agents embedded in the Federal bureaucracy."

"The ranking Vanguard officer on-scene, Colonel Malweise Baker, has indicated that they appear to have no equipment that might pose a threat to our forces. However, they are taking hostages and are armed and dangerous to the civilians they threaten as well as the community police who are seeking to facilitate their safe release."

"We believe the Machiavellians are targeting the public mostly as a diversion, intending to disorient and divert our efforts while they run an espionage operation in the National Archives."

"If they can successfully gain access to our secure data stores inside the facility, we fear they may then be able to engineer our combat suit technology as well as other classified proprietary research and development. We have not been able to get a line in to the Archives, which suggests they have already dismantled the established security there as well."

"Until we can ensure that the data is secure, we have disabled Porta-COM technology across the planet and through high orbit so as to mitigate the risk of any unlicensed dissemination of classified material. In the meantime, your coms will operate on radio bandwidth, so be advised that long-range communicability will be significantly reduced during this operation."

"Please egress to the terminal for your designated flight team. Thank you. Dismissed." said the computational intelligence, and with that, its hologram likeness faded out of view.

The process of exiting the amphitheater seemed to take many times as long as entering. There was a palpable tension in the room, and the ordering of Vanguards seemed to unfold in a strange manner; halfway between fettered exigence and a bustling trepidation.

§VC

When Oni and Thea finally arrived to the sector K-10 hanger, Leveigh and Michael awaited them, the latter dangling a half-smoked blunt between his ring and little finger.

"Oni, Thea. You ready?" asked Michael. They nodded. "I hope so," he continued pensively. A huff of smoke burled from out his nostrils, "This is a major combat mission. Won't be as easy as the incident with the senator. Haven't seen a situation this dangerous since the von Galen affair."

Leveigh's head sunk low. "Do you think we're ready then?" he said.

Michael quelled his cigarette "You have the best training humankind has ever had to offer its warriors," he replied, "but no. None of us are ready. We'll just have to make do and keep moving forward."

Corporal Simoneau shrugged. "Let's go. The briefing hologram is earmarked priority one, so we'll need to be first to the egress terminal." And with this, the four Vanguards walked briskly to the nearest transport vessel, grey and muted, and situated themselves in its personnel bay. Engines churned the oxygen around their ship as they departed, Earthward bound.

The voice of Aeschylus' native intelligence chimed on the intercom on their descent.

"K10 Vanguard Squadron Theta, you have been selected as the primary on counterintelligence efforts inside the Archives. Your task will be to head-off attempts to access the sole entry-point to our secure data stores in the facility."

"Guarding the entry alone will not be sufficient—we have reason to believe that at least one Ravenous operative is on-sight at the Archives —codename Ravenous Claw. This combatant will undoubtedly have some strategy to access those stores which accounts for Vanguard presence.

"For reference—information on the members of the Ravenous order:

Claw—An elite soldier who wears a large, highly responsive mechanized apparatus.

Bow—A sniper and assassin effective at any range. Has several dozen confirmed peace-keeper kills tied to his name.

Thane—presumed Lieutenant general & figurehead of the Machiavellian forces.

Legion—mastermind behind the broad-scale activities of the insurgency. Legion has never been positively identified as an individual operative by our government."

"Further, none of the legal identities of these persons have been established."

"Remember—you have been selected due to the exceptional combined performance of your unit in combat and strategy simulations. Thank you for your courage, K10 Theta. Do whatever you must to ascertain the plans of the Machiavellians, and stop them."

"He expects too much of humanity's leadership—not where their intentions lie, but in their general capacities. We have soldiers for war, teachers for peace, and politicians for everything in-between. There is a reason for this order of things. Simply put—von Galen's head is in the clouds, completely oblivious to the torrential consequences of his ideas in our society today. He is a buffoon, and should be dismissed as such by anyone with common sense."

— Dietrich Merkl, *Remarks on the Arrogance of the Ethocrats*

§VIA

"Eject! Oni, get ou—" Leveigh's voice belted out against the screeching wind before they were pulled into the open air.

The world span. Oni's ears were ringing almost as hard as her head ached. The innards of the transport ship glowed a dim red, which was mostly overtaken by the light pouring through the gaping wreck of the ship's hull. A body, lifeless and tattered, was strewn across the far end of the vessel; caught on the ragged maw of the transport's mortal wound. Its flight suit was badly torn and charred.

"Oni… ni are y… ere? Love, pl…" Thea's voice faintly cooed, fuzzing through the constraints of range in radio transmission. "Get out o… there. You nee… ake it ou…"

The air pummeled the cabin with a brutal, rhythmic tenacity. Oni's vision came into focus. Centripetal force wrested her against the wall and ceiling of the ship as she fell with its wreckage. Weakly, she pressed her index finger on the nape of her shoulder blade. Her suit sprang into life, expanding the hemline of its collar into a full helmet and visor. Steady, reliable air kissed Oni's lips, and in a waking moment she pulled herself to the wall adjacent of the damaged portion of the hull. With one bounding yell, she vaulted, clearing far beyond the horizon of the ship's exterior and only some dozens of yardage from the ground.

The suit's aeronautics activated, and Oni entered a controlled fall. Landing on her fists and knee, she found herself in the city's botanical gardens, several meters past the entrance to a subterranean public transport station. Vegetation of several climates rounded park pathways in every direction: exotic potted plants, great wide ferns and coniferous trees surrounded her.

The wind rustled gently along the filters of her helmet, and the faint loamy scent of nature welcomed her. But for a moment, the distant echo of bullets flying through nearby concrete corridors were as of yet the only sign that this was not an ordinary day in Metropolis.

"I'm out," she replied on the radio coms before retracting her visor. But if anyone was on the other end, they certainly would not have heard her speak.

The collision was as tremendous as it was horrible. The transport ship, already structurally weakened from the gape in its hull, buckled into the shape of a blunted crescent as it slammed against the ground. The soil shuddered, flinging out around the ship in every direction. Underneath, concrete and contorted iron rebars plied along the wedge of the oblong ship, revealing the shadow of a chasm underneath.

"Come in K10 Theta. Are any of you out there?" said Oni, approaching the vessel. The coms were silent. "I have an emergency situation, possible civilian-"

With a screeching bound, a lone rocket pummeled through the air and into the front of the crash-landed ship.

The resulting explosion activated a defense protocol in the flight suit, and Oni was launched into the air and away from the volatility. The transport sank, sliding into the bowels of the tunnel below, and greeted by the screams of its occupants. Oni flew in after it, the sparks of her suit whipping through the sky like fireworks. Landing just before the ship, she struck its fuselage with all her might as it came within an arm's length of several locals.

The body of the vessel careened into the railway tunnel. The energy of the room was transformed; grace and silence filled that which was terror before them.

"RUN! Go on, get out of here!" Oni shouted, reaching her fingers out towards the stairwell. The stage cleared, as Oni hopped onto the tracks. With prolonged fortitude, she wrested the transport ship from out of the tunnel. "Computer, geotag this station as out of commission pending repairs." Oni said.

"*Station marked.*" the A.I. answered.

As the remains of the shuttle rolled onto the platform, Oni turned to look down the line. The clammer of the stage-rubble had subsided, but it was replaced; by nothing calamitous, only the gentle shoe-tapping of a lone source some distance along the tracks.

Peering down the length of the tunnel, Oni saw a distant silhouette facing the adjacent wall. "Enhance optics." she said. Her visor's field-of-view adjusted to the sight of a man in a long coat and wide-brimmed hat stepping past the threshold of an adjoining opening in the wall which remained mostly out of sight. Something hung by his waist, but in the darkness, it had not been clear to her.

With a running start, Oni leapt, rocketing to the site of the mysterious figure. The musty air grazed her face with an unsettled stiffness; dust and mildew brushing the length of the stonework of the tunnel as she came. The entrance was one of several, but only the one was unboarded: its respective wooden planks torn from their place, splayed along the ground. An opaque windowpane was set along the top half of its door, on which were the words "For The Lady", though the first word was faded almost past the point of recognizability.

The sound of smashing tile and cement pounded through the space between the door, which trembled at the force of its causing. Oni grabbed the handle and entered.

Standing across the washroom and facing opposite was the figure she'd seen a moment before; standing with legs wide apart and a great hammer held head-down with the length of it pressed against the hind of his waist. Cement particulates floated chest-high between them, and the far wall had collapsed, revealing a large sewage tunnel behind it.

"Stay where you are." warned Oni.

"Oni." replied Corvin, turning his head. "Not a good time."

Oni blinked. "How did—", she started, but Corvin interjected.

"Read a file somewhere, I'm sure you'll imagine. . . for a while." As he faced Oni, the hammer evaporated in a whirl of smoke, which was dark as jade-stone under a moonless night.

Oni stared wide-eyed for a moment before regaining composure. "I'm taking you into my custody. We'll be walking up to the surface where my drop ship will meet us to collect and bring you to a secure facility for questioning." she explained.

Corvin turned back towards the sewers.

"Don't," Oni warned. "Lives are on the line right now, and I am authorized to use force if necessary. I cannot promise that you will remain uninjured if you disregard my instructions."

"Well," Corvin demurred, "if that's your intention, I suppose this will be the best for both of us." He stepped forward.

"Thank you." Oni replied, turning to walk back towards the train tracks.

Corvin jumped backwards with a preternatural swiftness, and all the dust and wreckage in the room shot up behind him, configuring itself into the wall's uninjured state.

Oni bounded, slamming her fist into the wall. Again, and again. Once the hole was wide enough, she plied her fingers along its contours and pushed. The concrete tumbled outwards. Only the briefest of moments had passed, but no sign of the peacoat man was present by the time Oni dropped onto the sewer's landing.

§VIB

"What the fuck was that?" said Oni, shrugging her brow. The tunnel was overbearing to each of her senses, and held no answers. Only the echoed little nothings of all that the sewer held rang true to her presently.

"Oni, is that you? Where are you? What's happening?" Thea's voice intoned over the radio.

Oni replied with an instinctive quickness, "Thea! I'm here. I'm in the sewer tunnels, tracking an unknown operative who seems to be making his way to the Archives with unidentified and dangerous technology. Possibly Legion? I'm not sure. What's going on with the rest of you?" she said, walking down the tunnel. Her visor indicated progress towards her destination.

"Leveigh and I are in the Archives. We've taken down all proximous threats, but still no sign of Ravenous activity. Oni... You should know, Michael—"

"I know," said Oni, "I saw his remains before I escaped from the ship. I don't understand—How is that possible? Doesn't our ship have the same tech as our suits? We should have all been safe."

There was a space of solemn quiet before Thea replied, "analysis indicates a timed electro-magnetic pulse milliseconds before impact. So far, I can confirm that the new tech is not integrated into their rank-and-file artillery. We've been targeted by sustained heavy fire without any injury during our activities on-the-ground... But at least to some degree, it seems they have the capacity to beat our defenses now. That must be why they've come out in the open after all this time..."

Oni nodded, "I concur. I'm heading in your direction and will submerge shortly. If we can get close enough to confirm that the data has not been breached, then we can employ thermal sensors to ensure no one gets—"

"Any last words love?" a gruff voice interjected over the coms, followed by Thea's. "He's here Oni. Come quickly." she said, and after a few seconds of clammer sounded over the speakers, the output fell silent.

Oni jetted forward along the length of the tunnel. "Computer," she stated curtly, "display schematics for the sewers, Archives, and populate it with the whereabouts of surviving K10 Theta members as soon as that information is available."

"*Understood.*" the A.I. replied. "*Data incoming. Generating schematics with coordinates for your unit now.*"

After weaving through the labyrinthine passages with great urgency, Oni Anagonye shot through a manhole, grasping the grate as she flew skywards. She looked around. Every angle was sparkling plexiglass.

She tossed the iron circular disc with pre-calculated instinct the moment she saw. Thea and Leveigh stood on either side of an imposing presence; their arms raised, suits ragged, and faces brutalized. The grate partially embedded in the window, having been caught in the tower's shatter-resistant facade. Oni launched forwards and slammed into it with a tenacious ferocity, forcing the iron sewer grate through the glass as she vaulted her way into the conflict.

The figure in the middle of the room was three-yards height, with bulky hydraulics bolstering a vaguely humanoid frame. The armor plating was dark grey and iridescent, with a large red illuminated strand along its visor and a great pincering pair of mechanical arms equipped with long, thin, claw-like fingers. And, on its chest was a subtle emblem; a raven in mid-flight.

Oni took no delay in her attack, and the Ravenous operative Claw faltered as she managed to place her hands on his chest and neck. Pulling a thick band of hydraulic tubing with the former hand as she pushed on the latter, she gouged and tore it as if it were a mere thread of delicate wicker lattice. Pounding her lower fist into his throat, she punctured the casing of the suit.

Moving her arms into position to tear out the chest of it, Claw rebounded, holding the length of her back with a singular grasp as he rammed her into the far drywall.

Oni collapsed. The adrenaline from all that transpired had been a powerful motivating force, but in the wake of this additional injury, the ringing ears and blurry vision returned with dire omnipresence in her conscious being. The sound of struggle behind her was cognitively distant, and when it had faded, Oni felt the sharp, long spear-like grasp entangle her frame once more.

"Ah, I see." Claw breathed, his mechanical grip adjusting as he hoisted her up against the wall once more, "your suit hardens as it encounters impact or pressure. You ethocrats are so terribly important… What a horror it would be if you were to find yourself…"

Snap.

"... vulnerable, like the rest of us."

The moment Oni's suit powered down, a shot rang out from behind her. In her last moment of consciousness, she found herself as if at the bottom of a lake—desperate for air.

"The trouble with which philosophy has always struggled is the business of discovering what things must be passed over in silence. This problem plays out in two major ways: In its theoretical dimension, the question centers on (as Kant so wisely asked) 'are we discussing that which is beyond the boundaries of all possible experience?'"

"But the practical dimension… These are the questions which plague our minds and haunt our dreams. 'Shall I revive a loved one, only to have them suffer death all over again?' or, 'Do I labor to restore the humanity of he who murdered my beloved?' The difference, of course, is that in the theoretical case, it is the doer who must be silent; whereas in the practical case, it is everyone but the doer."

— Edgar von Galen, *In and For*

Chapter Seven

§VIIA

The mist rolled gently along still water in the heart of a dawning morn. Oni yawned. Wind lingered in the berth of every tree along a narrow lake. A loon called out, but all else was at rest, and with every shallow breath Oni fell deeper into the trance of this serene autumnal visage.

"It's beautiful," said Corvin, walking up from behind her. "But you can't stay here, you know that. It's not your time yet."

The wisps of fog glided silently before them like cotton tufts drifting above an opalescent mirror. Oni's shoulders tucked forward, diving her pressed hands between her feet as she leaned into the earth. "Don't make me go back, please. The pain... it's—"

"Horrific, yes." Corvin finished, "True agony is ingeniously incomprehensible, even when one is in the midst of it. I'm sorry you've had to endure this, but without it you're not wholly yourself yet. The world cannot bear to wait until you are ready. Time marches

ever onward, always with indifference to our fears and sufferings. That is the cost of living I'm afraid. We all wind up like this in the end."
 Oni gasped for breath. She touched her lips as if reaching for a ledge. Corvin frowned.

"I am not omnipotent, you know." he said. "Not omni-anything really. If I were, or if anyone were, I don't know that this kind of suffering would be possible. Even I cannot prevent this. I am sorry for it."

Oni closed her eyes and envisioned the air entering her lungs. "I... I don't understand."

"And that's okay," Corvin replied. "Some things are not about understanding. The question is not always whether or not something can be understood; sometimes you can only reckon with the knowledge already in front of you. Let me show you something."

Corvin lifted Oni by the shoulders, cradling her as they walked down onto the edge of the water.

"I can't," she groaned, but held tight as he supported her way to its edge. They sat together.

"Suppose this lake is Creation." Ratzinger began. "We're not making any leaps here about its causing. No religious or secular commitments. It's just all that is in front of you as we contemplate in this moment."

Oni nodded gently.

"Look into its depths." Corvin invited. "How much do you see? What are its qualities? You're clinging to survival; perhaps this alters your motivation. Perhaps that too is instructive." He reached for a nearby branch and prodded it into the water.

"The light... distorts the wood as it enters the water." said Oni, "This is Descartes. I've read *First Philosophy*. Is this really the best time for — to discuss that? I can't seem to get enough air."

"There isn't time for anything else I'm afraid," Corvin answered, stirring the water, "You made a good connection to Descartes there, but let's take it a step further. Look again. Tell me what you see."

Oni gazed into the depths of the lake before her. As the surface troubled, the view below became obscured and the choppy sight of her own reflection came to the forefront of her attention.

"Me," said Oni. "I see myself."

Corvin nodded. "And thus spake Narcissus." he said. Oni furled her brow, and Corvin laughed. "Not a worry. We're putting you in the shoes of every person here. I'm not taking aim at you specifically."

Oni shuddered, grasping her chest with a wince.

"Let me get to the point." Corvin said, "Stirring the waters... This is what we do by engaging with the world around us. It's inescapable. It's the cost of our understanding. When we speak and come to think of an object in a certain way, the manifold relationality of our consciousness imprints the human patterns of reason indelibly into our experience."

"All encounters of the world are not merely receptivity to that which is real, but are rather inescapably an experience of our intimate bondedness to this nature. The world is out there, but the fundamental character of our relationship with it is constrained to the faculties of reason and the limits and fallibility of our senses. You're a Kantian. You know all this already."

"But what I don't think you realize is the cost of this truth in your daily life. The instrument of how you organize society, your precious 'democracy'... It assumes a uniformity of this encounterance, as if some universal anthropological principle were at the heart of all experience. Both the old world's government and yours calcify the shape of humanness in your own image. This is the fever-state of civilization. Yours is a compassionate dogma, but it is still dogma. It is greater than the moral sum of all societies before it, but it too must be overcome."

Oni sat in thought for a moment. "I appreciate your perspective," with a gentle gasp, she answered "but that's nonsense. Sorry."

Corvin's eyebrows floated high, "Oh?"

"Let's consider this reflection once more," said Oni. "When you look into the water, and you see your own reflection… your obligation to moral contemplation doesn't end there, recognizing the uniqueness of your fingerprint as you encounter the world."

"The reflection isn't just 'you-ness'. It's a reminder of the reality of otherness—it's seeing yourself as you are seen by others, as a body in existence. Yet when you see that body, you know it relates indissolubly to your own conscious self."

"You know that it represents the image of a person, and since that person is you, there can be no doubt in your mind that the image your reflection represents is that of an individual who is sensitive to the moral whims of her peers. And so it is in the case of other people when we encounter them. Do you understand? This is the very ground of empathy."

"I think you're right to see where this psychological phenomenon might lead us astray in our theoretical philosophy; much of our history's misery is rooted in the dogmatism of people incognizant of the limitations of human reason."

"However, there is no way to guarantee the well-being of the many without a strong system for organizing our resources and the judicious administration of our cultural and material wealth. Everything you've said—to me, all it points towards is the urgency of our need for an Ethocratic government, not its undoing."

Corvin nodded. "And so our struggle begins, Oni Anagonye. I am honored to be your adversary in this great conflict. The next time we meet, I may very well be forced to overcome you. But for now, all you need to do is—"

"BREATHE!" shouted a shaky baritone voice. Light swelled into Oni's eyes until all was white as snow. Whether she was too warm or too cold was indiscernible to her, as was much of her surroundings. Her vision blurred. Someone out of sight cried in terror. "Come on! You got this girl, you can do this. Just hang in there for me okay?" the baritone voice implored, clinging to the face of a small woman in medical scrubs.

Oni's breath condensed on the face mask, aromating its oxygen with the lingering dewey scent of her transcendental wanderlust. "Bring... me home." she whispered, and then fell to rest.

§VIIB

 Leveigh and Thea sat in the waiting-room. Bustling traffic and the muffled diction of the intercoms and medical staff floated like dust around them. Leveigh was seated at the edge of a chair, his elbows planted square on his knees, head held in the clasp of his hands.

Thea held her fingers in a ball to her forehead and whispered, "Sustainer of humanity—remove this illness, and cure her disease. You are the one who cures. Grant us a cure that leaves no illness, Al-'Adheem."

Leveigh turned his head. "Oh... I didn't realize you—"

Thea raised her hand, "I'm not. But it is her mother's tradition, and so I honor it as best their family taught me. It was their truth; It is what they would have done."

Leveigh nodded, and they sat in silence for a moment before he spoke again. "Does her mother know? God—I'm not even sure she'd want to tell her... What about Dawud?"

"Dawud is on his way," Thea replied, "and yeah—she wouldn't want her mother here. I'm going to call her if it starts looking like—" she trailed off, stifling the distress in her heart.

"Hey," Leveigh offered, coming to Thea's side, "hey, it's okay. They have some of the best doctors in the world here. She's going to make it through."

"Leveigh," said Thea, "How are we even here? There's so much that I don't understand right now. What happened? One moment, we were battered and overcome by the Ravenous operative. Next..."

"That man with the hammer, he came out of nowhere, fought Claw back and then—"

"And then suddenly we were at the doorsteps of the best hospital... in Prague." Leveigh finished, "I'm just as confused as you are. None of this makes sense. We're over 300 kilometers away from the conflict, and it happened in an instant... Several thousandths of a second according to my suit's flight data. That's..."

"Approaching the speed of light. I know, I checked too." said Thea. "It doesn't feel like we 'travelled' though. He came in, threw his hammer at Claw, turned his head and then... blinked, and we were here. That's not travel in any ordinary sense, is it? I think that may have been..." Leveigh's eyebrow furled.

"Don't look at me like that!" Thea pleaded, "I know it sounds crazy, but it's no more impossible than the idea that he could somehow move us with such incredible speed unharmed."

"That's speculation." said Leveigh, "Let's not go there now. We'll figure this out at a better time. We're in no position to find satisfactory answers to this yet."

"Yeah you're right... I'm just rattled. Easier to think about this than what's happening right now, I guess," she took a deep breath.

"Leveigh, I can't do this. If she goes, then my heart... I can't I—just can't say goodbye okay?"

Leveigh held his dear friend. "I know," he said, "I hear you."

§VIIC

The hospital room spun into recognition as Oni opened her eyes. The space around her swelled. Colors shimmered on the depths of her surroundings, and water clung to the skin of it. Of her. Her mind was muddled. There was a sound like the ocean, but it came in sporadic bursts of overwhelming presentness only to dissipate as quickly as it formed. Again and again it plagued her. A bodied-face floated to her bedside.

"Oni, it's me Dawud. How are you doing? Thank God you are okay." the face said, its frown locked into the presence of its personhood.

She tried to form words, though hadn't any thoughts to say. The vocal dispersions were birthed still-born until she regained a sense of her surroundings. "Brother?" She managed.

Dawud sat at her bedside. "Oni, the doctors say you're having ICU psychosis due to the stress this injury has put on your body and mind this last week. I'm not sure if you understand what's happening. Your brother is gone, but you are my sister in any way that matters to me, okay? I'm here for you."

Oni sat up. "The walls," she said, "they're pulsing… dripping… I can't… stop them." Her expression was fraught with fear and trembling.

Mr. Makgoba pulled the handkerchief from out of his breast pocket. "Your body is fighting an infection caused by your injury last week."

He wiped her brow, and reached for a glass of water at her bedside. "The supervisor asked me to make sure you hydrate. Drink up Oni. Let's get you home soon."

Oni took the glass. "No. Can't go back there. Not at home in myself anymore."

Dawud shook his head, "I don't mean back to your mom. You can stay with me until you feel better, or I'm sure the state will arrange for accommodations. Prague is wonderful. You'll love it here, once you're well enough to enjoy it."

Oni nodded, and shut her eyes.

A knock tapped gently against the door. "Come in," called Dawud. A gloved hand pried the door quietly from its frame, and in stepped an unexpected face. The man was thin and pale, with a jaw that was sharp as cut glass and a marbled stare. His wispy straw hair was coarse and balefully wrangled into submission.

"Hello," the man answered as he closed the door behind him. "My name is Heathrow Wilson. I wanted to check in on my colleague and see if she's recovering alright."

Dawud nodded, "Senator Wilson. It's an honor to make your acquaintance."

Heathrow nodded graciously. "You must be Dawud. Oni has shared a lot about you on her public logs. I'm sure the honor is mine." he offered, extending his hand. Dawud met his grasp eagerly with a grin. "So Mr. Makgoba, how is she?"

Dawud's smile faded. "She's... been through a lot. She's probably going to recover, unless the pneumonia worsens. The operation to remove the bullet and repair her lung was a success."

"She'll need a week or two of physical therapy before she is fully service-ready again, but the doctors caution that there's no knowing how long she'll need to recover enough from the psychological trauma to be ready to serve. Everyone processes this sort of event differently. Right now, she needs rest, so I was just about to leave her to it. Would you care to join me for some lunch?"

Heathrow hesitated. "Is it okay to just leave her here? What if she..."

"Needs us?" Dawud asked. He shook his head affably, "Do not worry friend. She is in excellent hands. She is at rest, and the best thing we can do right now is take care of ourselves well enough to be here for her when she's ready to have us."

"Alright," said the Senator. "Let's go get something to eat then, shall we?"

§VIID

A car swerved onto the ramp walkway of the old UCT private academic hospital. Oni careened out from the driver's-side door and into the emergency center. A mild green light flashed as she passed the entrance and an artificial voice chimed, "*identity authenticated.*"

"Where are they?" Oni begged the administrative assistant at the front desk.

"The ones who just came in?" the man asked. Oni nodded. "Sorry," he replied, "I know this is hard. Take a seat and the doctor will be with you shortly."

Oni sat down, and the desk clerk brought her a cup of water. "Drink up hun, it's always best to hydrate when you're in shock." He bundled her in a large cotton blanket.

"Are they okay?" Oni asked. "Did you see?"

The clerk shook his head. "I don't know… sorry ma'am. They ran the two of them straight in as soon as they got here. You'll know as soon as there is something to know."

"Two?" Oni said, brow furled. "There should have been three. Are you sure…?"

He grasped Oni's shoulder. "Ms…"

"Anagonye." Oni finished.

"Ms. Anagonye," the clerk offered, "I really can't say anything for certain. Please wait here and try to remain calm until our—"

As the man spoke, a civilian peacekeeper in uniform entered the building and approached the pair of them.

"Excuse me ma'am. Are you Oni Anagonye, seventeen and of 490 Prospect Street?" Oni blinked.

"Yes… I'm afraid I need to ask you some questions about your family. The state has opened an inquiry into the events of this evening. Here is our card," said the peacekeeper, furnishing an ivory-tinged slip from his pocket. "When you have finished tending to the immediate needs of your family, we look forward to your prompt attendance for questioning."

Oni's legs skittered about the footplates of her wheelchair. "I'm ready to go. I don't need this chair, I'm sure someone upstairs could use it more than me."

Dawud nodded. "It's just standard protocol. When you leave the hospital after a serious illness, you get a chair. That's the deal."

Oni peered up at her old friend. "The deal?" she demurred, "doesn't that imply I had a say in it?"

He laughed. "Can we go back to when you were talking about the walls doing weird stuff again? 'Cause. Uh. I got in less trouble with you back there." Dawud said, pointing his thumb up the stairs. Oni stuck her tongue out and grimaced playfully.

Heathrow's voice echoed from outside the front doors of the hospital, wiggling through the space of their conversation. "Today, we gather to honor someone truly remarkable. All make sacrifices so that the many will thrive in our society, but when—"

Oni sighed. "This is so embarrassing."

"Why?" Dawud responded, "you did a great thing, and were badly injured trying to save the lives of your friends. This is nothing to be embarrassed or self-conscious about."

Senator Wilson's voice perked through the conversation again.

"Without a second's hesitation, she leapt into a scenario she knew meant almost certain death. Not just for the sake of her colleagues, not just for keeping the peace, but so that the righteousness of our modern Union will remain ever the strongest of bonds."

Oni feigned a puking expression. Dawud snorted.

"Of course it's a Senator giving my introduction," she said.

"Hey, he came here to check in on you even though he doesn't know you," Dawud offered pointedly, "and like, he saw you poop in your hospital bed on several occasions and still talks about his admiration for you. He may be a rhetorician, but his care is genuine."

Oni's face disappeared into her hand. "Christ."

"And without further ceremony," Heathrow's voice interjected once more, "let me introduce to you the brilliant, graceful, and courageous Oni Anagonye, who has now been elevated to the rank of Captain aboard the Aeschylus, and shall henceforth be regarded as an official spokesperson for the Ethocratic state."

Her amused discomposure transformed into surprise. She looked at Dawud, and pointed at herself. Mr. Makgoba nodded, smiling, and pushed her chair gently out into the sight of the public.

"The hardest part of being human is to embrace a simple yet confounding truth—that is, that we all become who we are. No matter how someone has wronged us, no matter how frustrating or upsetting a person's actions are: monsters aren't real, and nothing occurs without causing. Through all the pain that living with others might bring us, we have the eternity of the grave to move on. Life is the only time we have for working through the ways in which we fail one another. If that is our end, then we must build a society which earnestly reflects this in its laws and institutions for every part of human existence."

— Edgar von Galen, *The Ethocracy*

Chapter Eight

§VIIIA

"Do you know why you're here?" Oni asked, facing the vista of the Prague skyline from under a stone arch. It was midday, and the cool breeze was a warm welcome—she'd worked up a mild sweat wheeling herself up to this view, and she was not about to look consternated or distressed in front of such a person.

"Prague Castle?" the man behind her asked.

Oni shook her head. "No, not Prague Castle. Do you know why you've been summoned to meet me?" The man stood in silence through Oni's invitation to reply. When none came, she continued, "We both know the answer, I just wanted to give you the chance to take ownership of your actions here."

"So that we're on the same page: you have been brought to me because your peers caught you drawing a swastika on the face of the Maisel Synagogue. The people saw fit to remit you into my custody because there is a belief in our society that, on occasion, even persons such as yourself can learn to do better. But can I be honest with you?" Oni asked, turning her chair to face him.

"By all means." The Nazi answered.

"I felt ill the moment they asked this of me," said Oni. "Like I was an inch from losing my lunch."

The man narrowed his gaze. "You think I care?"

Oni shook her head. "Of course not. I'm not white or a man, and you've decided that this means that somehow I am your inferior. People who draw swastikas for fun aren't known to be very empathetic. Gaining your sympathy was not my intention. I just want you to understand that were I listening to my gut, you would be at the mercy of the courts right now."

"The community you've injured and a panel of ethicists would be collaborating to derive a resolution to your case, and when all parties were satisfied, you'd face whatever consequences they'd require. Fortunately for you, the congregants of the Maisel Synagogue elected to forgo their rights in this case once they were made aware of my residence here."

The man puffed out his chest. "Yeah? And what makes you special?"

Oni signaled for his presence beside her at the balcony. He swaggered over to join her.

"When the Nazis came to Prague in 1939, Hitler spent a night in this castle," Oni began. "He stood on this balcony and surveyed his party's newest possession with great satisfaction. Do you know why we're here, Martin?"

He leaned back. "Yeah. We've been over that, you annoying bitch."

Oni lifted a finger up casually. "You don't want to know what happens if you call me a bitch again... And no, this time I mean something different: why we're in Prague Castle."

Martin shrugged, exasperated.

"We're here because I decided to bring you here. You like Nazis? Welcome to the place where their leader decided to own this city; a man of seemingly infinite power and influence in his heyday. Today, after hearing of your case, I petitioned the municipal board and they granted me sole purview of this castle during the remainder of my recovery."

"Hitler died in paranoia and despair. When I look out on beautiful Prague, I see a politically, economically, and intellectually freed people. And they are all in my care." She looked Martin square in the eyes. "So I want you to pay close attention when I remind you that I'm with the people who replaced those governments which, in their limelight, managed to pry Prague from Hitler's cold, dead fingers."

Martin sneered. "Weren't they the good guys in that quaint narrative? What are you saying... that your government upended the anti-Nazi agenda? I guess we're not so different in our aims after all, huh?"

Oni's brow flew skywards, but in a moment her face relented as she recited Sartrean verse.

"'Never believe that anti-Semites are completely unaware of the absurdity of their replies. They know that their remarks are frivolous, open to challenge. But they are amusing themselves, for it is their adversary who is obliged to use words responsibly, since she believes in words.'"

"The anti-Semites like to play with discourse for, by giving ridiculous reasons, they seem to discredit the seriousness of their interlocutors. They delight in acting in bad faith, since they seek not to repudiate by sound argument, but to intimidate and disconcert.' That's Sartre, if you were wondering, which you weren't."

The Nazi bared his knuckles. "You want to know who you're messing with, bitch? I'll fuck you up past—"

Oni snapped her fingers. Her suit flew out from behind some drapery and restrained Martin's arm as he raised it. "Computer," Oni intoned, "please escort our guest to a more amenable position."

§VIIIB

"Hey," Martin yelled, "get your hands off me! You can't—" but before he could complete his thought, the suit unfurled itself as if into parchment and wrapped its contours along Martin's body, until he was its new occupant.

Then, without circumstance, the suit marched him over to the balcony and sat him in full view of his teacher. Cheekily, the AI placed his head upon the palms of his hands, elbows planted along the height of his legs, and a smiley face was then displayed along the visor of the suit.

"Oh look," Oni grinned, "a captive audience!"

The AI chimed in with its usual cheery intonations, *"ready and eager to learn, Ms. Anagonye!"*

"You're the worst," Martin said, his voice thinned and muffled from a suit that would not project his voice.

"I warned you not to call me 'bitch' again." Oni reminded him with a smirk. "But here's the rub: you think I loathe you because you have all this hatred and anger in your heart. I don't. Martin, no one is out to get you. I want for you what I want for any person to have—a life full of joy, tenderness, expression, thoughtfulness, and a sense of belonging; but so long as you believe in these lies, you will always find your progress to well-being frustrated through the vicissitudes that these feelings bring. I've looked at your personnel file... You are a painter, I believe?"

Martin's head nodded. "Just to be clear," he said. "That was the suit nodding. Not me." The smiley face on his visor briefly seemed to stick a tongue out.

"Then let's get you into some painting classes, and school to study aesthetic theory." Oni offered, "In the meantime, here's what's going to happen. You're going to attend a series of listening sessions for Jewish people who have been the victims of hate crimes. You will record a video diary of your thoughts and feelings after each of these sessions."

"Once the community to which you have been assigned releases you, you will then attend therapy until your rehabilitation supervisor believes you have resolved these issues. Until then, they will be your constant companion and for all legal purposes your sole custodian. Upon graduating from this program, you will be asked to paint a portrait that encapsulates the meaning of this journey for you. Commit another hate crime, and you will be blacklisted, never to enjoy the fruits of the Ethocracy ever again. Do we have an understanding Martin?"

The visor opened to a gently tear-stained face. "Yeah... okay. I'll try."

Oni started wheeling herself towards the door. "Humor is a way of disarming one's own anguish," she began. "I want you to know—even though you did not do this to me, my heart aches for the community you've wounded."

"I hope you take seriously the urgency of your assignment here: society cannot permit your way of being-in-the-world. We will be watching you closely. I hope for your own sake that you invest heavily in finding a way to make this journey authentic for you. Otherwise, you will die full of hate, alone and without any outlet for expression. Welcome to your *purgatorium*, Martin Kempf." She opened the door, gesturing for his exit.

"I pray you make the most of it."

"Be not afeard. The isle is full of noises, sounds, and sweet airs that give delight and hurt not. Sometimes a thousand twanging instruments will hum about mine ears, and sometime voices that, if I then had waked after long sleep, will make me sleep again. And then, in dreaming, the clouds methought would open and show riches ready to drop upon me, that when I waked, I cried to dream again."

— Caliban, Shakespeare's *Tempest*

Chapter Nine

8IXA

Oni and Heathrow sat in a drawing room. The polished floor flickered from the light of candles along each arch of the gothic style. Soft brightness illuminated several delicate stonework ridges along the cathedral ceiling, which adorned a line of cast-iron chandeliers along the length of it.

An automaton in the corner serenaded them with the live performance of a Bachian cello suite. Rain tapped against the window panes as Heathrow reached for his glass of zinfandel.

"They breached it, didn't they?" said Oni.

Heathrow nodded. "Yes, they did. We logged two successful access attempts. A DarkNet protocol was activated on the second pass, so we don't know what was gleaned from that endeavor. The first read was a server log recorded with screen capture."

"The information was quantum-encrypted, so genetic algorithms aren't a risk for data breach. They will either need a quorum of Vanguards to access the data, or technology the likes of which we cannot even comprehend."

Oni blinked. "And what if someone had that capability?"

"Well," replied Heathrow, "then let's hope they aren't Machiavellian. If they are, we might have a war on our hands."

"A war?" asked Oni, incredulous. "We'd have trouble to be sure. Big trouble. But do you really foresee insurrection as a possible consequence? I'm sure the public feels as violated as we do. The Machiavellians are many things, but numerous is not one of them."

Heathrow sat forward from his chair. "Do you know that?" he asked.

"No," said Oni, "it's an educated guess from the public polling we've seen regarding our performance as their government. Only seventeen percent of respondents have ever shown dissatisfaction with our work, and to presume that even a large fraction of those are thereby working to undo the State… it's not likely, is it?"

Heathrow took a sip of wine. "No," he said. "I suppose not. But then again, we would have considered last month's events impossible—right up until they happened."

Oni demurred. "Impossible? Never." she said. "Did we predict it? No… but it was predictable. We just missed the significant factors which would have indicated its eventuality to us."

The young Senator turned his head. "Factors such as?"

"Heathrow, listen," Oni replied, "We must never come to believe that because our manner of thought was unable to anticipate the development of new tyrannies, that these fiendish ideations were somehow always and inexorably beyond our grasp. Our thinking was wrong. Let's accept that, and try to find out how. I'm not saying I have the answers. I'm saying the answers are out there."

Thunder beckoned their attention, rolling in the distance. The rain had softened just when the light of day grew faint.

"Perhaps you are right." said Heathrow. "Hopefully the Senate investigation will turn up something of consequence. But so long as their leader Ravenous Legion remains under our radar, I'm unsure of what progress can be made. In the meantime, you mentioned to my staff that you urgently wished to speak to me... What is it, Captain?"

Oni breathed deeply. "During the operation... in Old Wien... there was a man. He did some things that I had assumed... were impossible. I suggest you personally review the feeds from K10 Theta's suit recordings."

"It's a lot to take in. . . I'm not sure what we're dealing with, or who he is. My instincts seem to fail me here. But he's potentially a threat to national security and the peace. We need to learn more about this man and find out what his aims are. I think... he was likely one of the two successful perpetrators of the server breach."

Senator Wilson stood up. "Yes, well. In the interest of global security, I had your feeds isolated for initial review before public release later this week. Standard protocol for incidents such as the battle for Metropolis. I'll do as you suggest, friend. I trust your judgement."

"As for Michael's feed—"

"Yes," Oni added, "not much of use there."

The Senator shook his head. "No, I imagine not... But it wouldn't have mattered: he elected to have his video feed turned off during the hour preceding his death. I just wanted to know: can you think of any reason he would have done such a thing?"

"Yeah," said Oni flatly, "the dumbass was smoking just before we flew out. High out of his mind, probably."

"Dumbass?" Heathrow inquired. "I should have thought you'd be glad that his final moments were relatively relaxed given the circumstances. I don't mean to pry—"

Oni interjected, "Yes, thank you."

Heathrow hesitated. "... well, I've read your file Oni. I know how your family died. So I understand why you might have strong feelings here. But I don't want you to be angry at Michael. We need you to give his eulogy at the funeral next week... do you think you can do that? Find peace with his last moments, that is?"

Oni barred her teeth, then relented. "If you've read my file, then you of all people can understand why I think substance abuse in situations of responsibility is egregious."

The Senator nodded. "Abuse? Absolutely. But is that what Corporal Kuhn did? He shouldn't have continued smoking once called for service, but he was off-duty that day. You know, the civilization from which the names of our flagships are derived—" Heathrow began to pontificate.

"The Greeks." Oni offered curtly.

"Yes," said Heathrow. "The Greeks believed that virtue could be found in the balance of every facet of human life."

Oni's eyes darted from side to side before meeting Heathrow's once more. "Do you... think I helped pick those names for the flagships or something? Not a huge fan of the literature from Ancient Greece. I mean sure Homer and Plato are good reads, but Aeschylus is overblown, Euripides is generic, Aristotle reads like a car manual,

Herodotus and Thucydides are flagrantly mastrabatory, and don't get me started on…"

"Yes," Heathrow adjourned. "I defer to your own aesthetic sensibilities, Oni. I just want you to remember his humanity."

Oni paused and dwelled in the coldness of that silence as the automaton finished its serenade. "Yes," she said. "How could I not? And besides... he was my friend."

The silence lingered. Oni sat up and grabbed her wine glass, filling it three fingers. "God," she whispered. "He was my friend."

§IXB

Michael and Oni sat on a picnic blanket on the crest of a rolling hill, meters from the wood-line below. The daze cast light through a Summer valley, and the gentle wind caressed their skin with the tender promise of a lingering warmth.

"Is Thea joining us?" Corporal Kuhn wondered.

Oni turned her head to meet her friend's gaze. "I dunno. She had said she was going to meet us up ahead, but I think she's running late."

"Well then," said Michael, "we'll just have to make do without her, won't we… You ready?"

"No, I don't think so." Oni replied.

Corporal Kuhn shook his head. "Me neither. Who would have ever thought it'd be down to us? And then when you've made it, I'll have to walk back alone…" There was a stoic composure to his voice.

"Yeah," said Oni. "I never thought about that. I'm sorry. Too much on my mind lately."

Michael smiled. "Well no worries. We've got a long ways to go before we get there. Shall we?" he said, offering his hand.

They walked down to the tree-line, and a tributary bustled into view as they crossed into the woodland—water ushering a chorus of splashing and rustled stone into the soundscape. They walked down the angled riverbank as they visited.

"She's eager to see you." Michael proffered. "I hope you know that."

Oni looked at the matted floor beneath her, stepping in its thick and pulpy dusting of scattered plant-matter. "I know," she said. "Normally I'd just say that I wish I could say the same. But you know, that's the solace of dreams: they never have to make sense, which is a relief to those for whom all the sense in the world is anathema."

The Corporal laughed. "You talk like that in your sleep?"

Oni's eyes narrowed. "Maybe… Shut up." Together, they crossed a narrow spread of the river, hopping along the loose stones dotting the breadth of it. Up ahead, the water forked along two paths: to the left, it ran deeper into the woodland, and rightwards it fanned out into a spread of yellow reeds.

"Which way?" Michael asked.

Oni pointed at the reeds. "You go out into the marshlands. I'll join you when I wake up. I think she wants to meet me alone."

He nodded, and quickly brisked his way out of sight. Oni sighed. Walking along the leftward waters, a pond came into view at the edge of the reedy wetlands. At the far end of it, a great boulder was wrapped in the thrall of enormous serpentine roots—ensigning the woman who sat on the height of it as the heir of what she surveyed.

Oni joined her mother, sitting on the stone with a view of their reflection in the water.

"You always loved looking for tadpoles in the water here." said Mrs. Anagonye.

"Yes," Oni replied. "Like with anything worth seeking; at first you just notice the environment, the water and the floor beneath. But then movement catches your eye and if you're quick enough, if you know how to focus your gaze in time, you catch sight of them. And the delight you feel in that moment makes the waiting worthwhile."

Her mother nodded. "Almost word for word what I said to you, fifteen years ago, love."

Oni's eyes welled with grief. "Why did you want me here mom?"

Mrs. Anagonye held her daughter close, tucking Oni's head underneath her chin. "To see my daughter. It's been too long. I've missed you."

Oni pulled away. "It's not this easy... No. Sorry. You know why I can't just..." she started. Pausing, she clenched her fists along her brow, crying.

"I know," her mother said. "My sorrow is no salve for you. I understand."

"But you don't have to forget in order to forgive. Dad and I—"

Oni interjected. "We all become who we are. I don't hold your past against you. Whether or not I know why your drinking problems began is irrelevant. We are human."

"As much as I miss my brother and father... I know you have been in hell ever since. I don't distance myself to add to that. I do it because I know that I will never be able to look you in the eyes without remembering that loss; and because… If I try to reconnect with you and fail, which is likely, you will be the worse for it, and I can't have that on my shoulders too."

Her mother caught her gaze. "We don't… know that your father is dead. What if he came back to us? Would you try then?"

Oni closed her eyes. "We do know though. The trail of blood shows that he walked right out into the river. It was freezing that night. Just because they didn't find his body… that doesn't mean he isn't gone."

Movement shimmered along the surface of the water in front of them.

"Dad?" Oni whimpered.

SIXC

"DAD!" she screamed, leaping straight-wise up from the comfort of her bed.

Thea woke swiftly, turning to hold her partner who was in the throes of panicked breaths.

"Hey, hey, it's okay, it was just a dream." she consoled Oni, pulling her close. "Shhhh, hey I've got you. I've got you Oni. I'm here. It's okay."

Oni began crying.

"Oh my love," said her companion. "Was it another dream about the accident?" Oni shook her head gently, "it wasn't an accident, she chose to drive drunk. Please don't call it an accident." she cried.

Thea rubbed her shoulders tenderly with one hand while cradling her head and neck in the other. "I won't anymore love. I promise." Thea replied. " Do you want to talk about it?"

Oni rubbed her nose. "No, it's just hard. Nothing new. Mom came to visit Dawud a few weeks ago, so I've been thinking about it more again." She held her head tightly. "I miss them so much, Thea. Sometimes I feel like I can't handle it. And I want to forgive her, but it just feels impossible and I don't know what to do." she whispered, stifling a sob.

Thea kissed Oni on the cheek. "It is impossible. Living through the deaths of your brother and father… I can't begin to imagine, even now. I'm so sorry Oni."

Thea's lover cried freely for some moments before her breath settled. "I'm so sorry." she whispered again, and then she too drifted back to sleep.

§IXD

A flash of red spanned the length of the room, followed by the dim roll of thunder. Oni awoke to the sight of Thea sitting on the cedar chest at the end of the bed, dressing up in the undergarments for her flight suit.

"Sorry to wake you dear." Thea cooed, "There's an emergency beacon emanating from the old church on the town square. Someone died, so I'm going to go check it out. You go back to sleep, okay? I want you to rest up, you deserve to get some sleep." she sat next to Oni on the bed, "I'll be back before you realize I'm gone." After a kiss on the brow, she left the room.

For a time, Oni shifted in and out of consciousness. Restless, she finally stirred. The thunderstorm had persisted. As she came to the bedside window, another flash filled the sky, and the drops of water on the glass shone for a moment like blood.

The lightning had been the source of this peculiar lustrous sight, but what caught Oni's immediate attention were the words: '*ONLY THE WORTHY*', which seemed as if they were carved out of the night sky itself, hanging above the Church of Our Lady Before Tyn. The red lightning struck once more. Then again—and again—around that house of worship.

"Computer," said Oni quietly. "Suit up."

The lightning died down, leaving the city in relative blackness. The power had fallen out, and only the moon, starlight, and words above the church granted any visibility. As she neared the square while flying above the rooftops, Oni whispered, "Computer, turn on low-light vision."

She hovered over the town square. "*Vision granted.*" the computer intoned as she landed.

Her face narrowed. All around her were statues of people… seeming to be in flight of some catastrophe around the church, and at each of their feet were scorch marks. Many seemed huddled in terror, shielding their faces with their arms or cowering leewards from the berth of the writing above the Church of Tyn's steeple.

She walked to the entrance of the vestibule. The doors hung open, and the echo of each step she took scattered to the corners of the high-arched ceiling. The candles flickered, their waxy scent admixed with dust and stone; but the vast open space of the cathedral was drowned out in the muted blue of nightfall.

She retracted her suit's helm. A shadow lurked along the front wall, harkening the sense of twisted wings; yet strewn across the stonework haphazardly, like the remnant shards of a broken stained-glass window. Attached to them at the head of the center altar was the All-Father.

"The name is Corvin, by the way," he called. "Corvin Elrick Ratzinger."

Oni continued walking forward. "I didn't ask," she replied.

Corvin grinned. "Oh, but you did," he replied. "You just don't say it out loud. But I know you Oni. I've seen more of your life than you have. You want answers. You always look for the answers—whether or not the questions make any sense."

"So," said Oni, bobbing her head, "is this why you brought me to Prague? For some grand demonstration of your power?"

Corvin rolled his eyes. "Don't be ridiculous," he answered. "I had to give you time to recover before our next meeting… and if I'm to wait, what better pass-time than the opera?"

"Did you know they're showing *Don Giovanni* at the Estates Theatre? I never got to see it as a boy… Wrong part of the map, no money to speak of… but I must have gone half a dozen times waiting for you! What a thrill." Corvin explained, exasperatedly drooping his arms at his sides.

His smirk returned with a bite. "I thought about inviting you… but I had a feeling you'd interrupt the show, since I'd have to try to kill you, and you're better than most humans at not dying."

Oni's heart sank in her chest. "Kill me?" she said, her heart racing. "why save my life just to end it now? And if you're going to end my life anyways, why not strike me down when I was weak? You've had ample opportunity to do it more easily than now."

Corvin blinked. "Yes. Well, perhaps you're right. Or, perhaps again, you misunderstand the point."

"Where is Thea?" Oni demanded, stepping towards her adversary. "Is she another one of your statues? If she is, I'd start praying that your self-confidence is not misplaced." Her words were muted, but delivered with a commandeering forcefulness.

The All-Father's shadow-wings collapsed like smoke, billowing into the shape of a great hammer in his hands. "She's where she needs to be," he replied. "As are you. And if I do kill you, I promise by my life that she's next. Now, show me your fury Oni Anagonye."

"If you need proof that what I'm saying is true, just look at the polls; it's not going to happen. If the liberal order can triumph over Aristocracy, Fascism, and Marxism—it sure as hell won't be defeated by these so-called Ethocrats. The nation-state and the market will prevail. They always do, and always will—and you can take that to the bank."

— Parliamentarian Mitch Bannon's BBC interview, one week before Old Britain's referendum concerning the legalization of Ethocratic conventions

Chapter Ten

§XA

Oni leapt, careening into Corvin like a comet darting across the night. He lurched, catching her fist with his own.

"Borrowed strength," he grunted. "I guess we have something in common after all. Too bad it's—" Corvin began, but was cut off and startled when the vents in the caught-arm of her suit protruded, spitting copious volumes of ignited jet fuel directly at his face. The blow-back shot her into the air, and set one of the neighboring altarpieces along the nearest pillar ablaze.

Corvin's pea coat appeared tattered and charred for but a moment. He stood tall through the whole of the attack, and seemed uninjured.

"You know," Oni pondered, as Corvin lowered his arm's defensive posture, "I wasn't sure whether or not you were something new until tonight. Everything of which you're capable... it's not from technology is it? You just withstood a... somewhat controlled blast at almost 1000 degrees celsius without being harmed. What are you, Corvin?"

The All-Father disappeared in a puff of black smoke and, in no matter of time whatsoever, Oni was inches away from the gaze of his silver eyes, the color of it shrouded in darkness and the declension of all inhibition. "Not. Something. New." Corvin rasped, and struck Oni into the pews at the far end of the cathedral; the lot of them clattering in a wreck.

With another swift reapparition—he grabbed her by the ankle, slamming her into the gold-and-black ornament of the next altarpiece some twenty meters distant—the fragmented woodwork splintering like glass.

Caught in the wreckage of it, Oni's eyes fixed on Corvin just in time to see him relinquish the handle of his weapon. The hammer soared, the head of it hurtling straight for her chest. Blue light flickered, and the object was brushed aside by the energy-shielding of her flight suit. Corvin cursed.

As he strode forward, Oni found her footing and flexed the remnants of the wood-stand apart. She ran at the All-Father, fist raised; yet just before reaching him she veered skywards, landing on the ledge of the organ wind-chest.

Prying two pipes from its frame, she sank her fingers deep into the metal, which crumpled like hollow aluminum underneath her grasp, the length of them protruding downwards. She vaulted towards Corvin, brandishing the metal cross-wise. Corvin raised his arms to fend off her assault.

Pirouetting mid-air, Oni landed in a curled ball at Corvin's feet, and with all her might shot upwards, smashing him on the underside of his chin. Corvin stumbled, but in a half-second his chest was skewered with two hunks of metal.

She slammed him against the pulpit, which toppled as she pushed the impromptu blades through him and embedded them into its frame. The All-Father lay motionless. Oni sat for a minute, watching Corvin's unblinking, aimless gaze. She checked his pulse along the windpipe, but found only stillness.

All was as silence.

"Great work." said Corvin, walking out from behind Oni.

"Jesus!" Oni yelled.

"No really—if I were mortal," he continued, gesturing sheepishly at his own corpse, "that... definitely would have killed me." the All-Father bit his lips. "Yikes." He waved a hand at the remains, which then evaporated in a deluge of smog.

Oni breathed in slowly, "so how does this play out? Are you going to kill me now? I have nothing. You win."

Corvin laughed. "If I actually wanted you dead, I'd have just transported us both into space and watched you boil in a cloud of your own blood," he offered helpfully.

Oni squinted. "Boiling is technically a cooling process. In a vacuum, that wouldn't do anything…"

"Eh," Corvin shrugged. "You'd still be dead. No, I just wanted to know what it would be like to fight you myself. What a pleasure, by the way. They really weren't kidding, what they wrote about you in your personnel file."

Oni frowned. "I mean fair enough, but I still don't understand the point of—my personnel file? That's a state secret. You… it *was* you that breached the Archives then. I knew it."

Corvin leaned in, "Yes, well. Someone had to. All sorts of naughty things, your government has been up to."

"You're joking." said Oni. Corvin shrugged his shoulders. "Well, coming from you I'm not sure what to make of that. You're no saint yourself, for one."

The All-Father looked at the ceiling. "You're right. Saints are the folk who do the bidding of their god. So I was hoping—" he dawdled, rolling his hand bemusedly.

Oni raised her finger towards the All-Father. "Let's get one thing clear. You may be a god for all I know, but you are not, and will never be, my god. That's a title reserved for no being. Got it?"

Corvin shook his head. "Of course, of course... That's not really what I had in mind for you anyway. Actually, I was thinking maybe—" he offered, placing his hand on her shoulders.

"You'd like to join me instead."

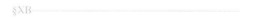

The world went dark. Everything was black as the raucous sound of chanting stirred to life.

Buddha, Mother, Dagda, Shadow, Mantra, Nouma, Bloodlife, Eliš,
Buddha, Mother, Dagda, Shadow, Mantra, Nouma, Bloodlife, Eliš,
Buddha, Mother, Dagda, Shadow, Mantra, Nouma, Bloodlife, Eliš,
Buddha...

"In the beginning was the Word," Corvin spoke quietly. Tendrils of light blossomed from a singular point some unfathomable distance ahead. As they exploded into view, the sound of the Light Eternal surged all around them. The coils of light coalesced into spiraled disks and ellipticals. "One brief sentence into the most widely-read account of the creation of the universe, and already they got it wrong."

The All-Father continued, "First, there was difference. Dialectic, if you will—the force of two poles across a single continuity. Fusion-forges in the heart of a million million stars gave us the elementary groundwork for everything that came next; the chemical complexity of the enumerated substances seeding exponential diversification among the world."

"Then came life, the first language, the secrets of its workings scrawled on banded molecules as if beckoning for its own awareness. Then speech, the second language, but the third order of difference— the third dimension of the cosmic dialectic. And now here we are, at the absolute limit of the Cosmos."

The light had swelled into a critical mass, and Oni could see that she and Corvin sat on the boulder from her childhood, planted in the roots of its tree, now staring at the virgin sky.

"This is my backyard." Oni whispered incuriously, "My backyard is the absolute limit of the Cosmos?"

"No," Corvin placated, "not your backyard. This conversation. World history has in it several key moments wherein a new and higher reality unfolds, communicating a richer, wholler grandeur through which it can find satisfaction in itself."

"The formation of stars, the first molecule of ribonucleic acid, the rise of humanity, and now... you. Just as each of these steps brought a new significance to all which came before it, our destiny together will beget a higher state of existence, depth of meaning, and wonder in the Universe."

"Us? Our destiny?" she inquired. "I don't really like you man. You're weird and creepy and you seem to be really fixated on violence."

"And yet." Corvin said.

Oni's eyes widened. "Hmm, okay… well… That's… a lot. Are you sure you even have the right person?" She balked. When Corvin nodded his head, her shoulders drooped.

"For what it's worth," Corvin offered, "death isn't quite the same sort of awful thing that humans seem to think it is. Killing is largely wrong and cruel, I'll grant you that… But it's more like stealing something priceless than destroying it forever. It's… complicated, but I'll explain how that all works too if you want."

Oni's arms dropped. She turned her head, "Are you serious? You're just answering all these questions? Most people spend their whole lives stressing out about these meanings of meanings and you're just going to dish them out like some sort of tele-marketed crash course? How do you even know this stuff?"

Corvin cupped his hand. "I might have fudged the whole 'not omniscient' thing. It kind of depends on how you define 'knowledge' as to whether or not it's true… but stuff that's reasonably called 'knowable'… I've *mostly* got you covered."

Oni stared off into space. "Okay. What happens when you die?"

Corvin sat up. "You cease to exist."

Oni pressed her face softly into the hold of her palm. "Yes, that's what a lot of us assumed. Thanks for that one Corvin, I'll file it under 'grand revelations' in my mind."

Corvin shook his head. "No, you're not listening. *You* cease to exist. Life, however, goes on."

Oni blinked.

"Okay," he continued. "Identity is important. All the greatest art and innovation, it sparked from the unique capacities of an individual mind thinking in concert with a community. The progress of world history needs that possibility, and so it exists—and thereby individual identity is born. But when it is extinguished, what remains? Life. The ground of your Being."

"It's not *you* anymore per-se, but it is *a* you. The finitude of the individual is indispensable for transformation, and so we must die in order for new and unbiased minds to be born and foster ever more profound genius into the eyes of the World. But that is *still us*."

"We may lose the sense of ourselves from life to life, but this is the great gift of our inheritance—that although we are eternal, we discover the magic of reality always and forever anew. There is a season for wonder, a season for growth, a season for engagement, and then a season to see what is next. And then the cycle renews itself. That is what happens when 'you' die."

"Okay," Oni meandered, "I think I understand what you're saying. But then what about you? You say you're a god. Does that not make you immortal? You suggested so earlier, and I must say; I think you made a pretty good case for it."

He laughed. "Corvin Ratzinger will die, when he is ready for it. However, the All-Father is Eternal, and that is the I *behind* this I. There are certain Beings that are as fundamental to the order of the world as light itself. I am vested with one of them. It has been given many names: Dagda, Yahweh, Odin, Zeus… and for now, Corvin. You may be another like Us, should you so desire, for I sense in you the power of a great Spirit, one worthy of the Light Eternal."

Oni shook her head, wide-eyed, "No, that sounds insane. Sorry. I guess it helps me make sense of some of what you've been up to, but like— you still killed those people."

Corvin waved his hand dismissively. "I didn't. They're back living their finite lives, blissfully unaware of what happened last night. Not a worry."

Oni's brow tightened. "While a relief, that's not as comforting as you seem to think it is."

Corvin placed his hand on Oni's. "I am not the monster you think I am, Oni Anagonye. Both of us will sacrifice much before the end of this. Let us be kind to one another."

"Okay... I still don't like you." Oni protested meekly.

"Yes, well, that's rather par for the course for us gods I'm afraid. See you soon." And with a slight gesture, the All-Father vanished.

Oni sat for a moment. "Did he just... Leave me here?"

"*It appears so, Oni.*" said her AI, "*Shall I send for your ship?*"

"The most pernicious quality of the Era of Subjugation was the way in which the ruling class of the time was able to convince large swaths of the population that they were being given the very things they were systematically denied—freedom, education, security, peace. The anathema of these was always perpetuated by the nation-state which was nominally honor-bound to guarantee them; for whatever use the concept of 'honor' has ever done mankind."

— Edgar von Galen, *The Ethocracy*

§XIA

"It wouldn't have made a difference you know." Heathrow whispered to Oni, the two of them sitting in the sacristy of the Cathedral of St. Vitus.

"Hmm?" said Oni.

"If he'd been sober… He would still have died either way." he offered.

Oni leaned forward. "I know. Today I don't feel angry. I just miss him."

Heathrow nodded. " I'm glad you've found peace."

Both their heads turned as, in the adjoining room, Amazing Grace filled the nave of the church. A choir luxuriated the palatial space, beckoning their attention.

"You ready?" asked Heathrow.

Oni, staring at the floor, stood up and walked out towards the chapel. When she arrived at the lectern beside the casket, she closed her eyes, took a deep breath, then spoke.

"It's hard to know where to begin, commemorating the life of a person like Michael. Born in Phoenix, the man was a beacon of kindness and generosity to all. And at first, all I could think about was how badly I wanted to express my rage at the people who stole him from us."

"And I would do only that for the rest of my days, would it stir but one atom of life back into him. But—" Oni shuddered. A brief pause for composure, and then she resumed. "That is not the way of things. And so we are left to mourn what has been taken from us. Michael was a caring friend, a brilliant philosopher and scientist, and a public servant in every sense of the phrase."

A hundred stained-glass windows suffused the space with their every majesty. Oni's breathing settled. The silence was tense no longer.

She cleared her throat. "In the course of a person's life, all manner of things must come to pass. And, in the wake of such a loss, we all wonder how to quell this unspeakable grief; hoping fervently for peace which surpasses all understanding."

"The road to that promised land is long and arduous; so far what I've learned is this—that even as our friend has passed from us, what remains is the very best of him: the care-taken whose lives were transformed by his service, descendants of the down-trodden whose ancestors' legacies have been vindicated by the work of the government to which Michael dedicated his life, and understudies who became their best through his mentorship."

"Now it is a natural impulse to get caught up in the lingering fear with which we all struggle yet scarcely mention: that while we live in community, all of us must die alone. But this thought, while understandable, is mistaken."

"If life were forever, charity would vanish; no stakes in the value of the life of the other would be sufficient. We sacrifice for one another because we don't take flourishing for granted in the finitude of individual existence. Though the maw of our mortality looms large over each of us, every possible tomorrow is a beacon in the darkness."

Oni looked at an open-faced watch which sat on the slanted surface of the pulpit. "If Michael ever gave you a new possible tomorrow, I invite you to now light your candles."

In the midst of the motion in the pews, daylight grew dim. The color drained from amidst each attendant. Oni continued, "Today, a shuttle simulates an eclipse over Central Europe so that our observatories can make new discoveries about solar systems whose line of visibility runs near the path to our Sun."

"This moment holds a very special place for us today, since Corporal Kuhn actually volunteered on the technology panel which originally advocated for the funding of this research project. His light, as the light which came through these beautiful mosaic window-panes, is now gone. And yet here we are, thousands of candles glimmering with the hope that he brought us." Oni said, her face glowing softly from the gold-tinged flame of her own possible tomorrow. Tears met a bittersweet smile.

"Michael didn't die alone. He only died to aloneness. What is left of him is an eternal belonging, as all the ways in which his goodness shaped each of us will echo through the ages long after every name here has been forgotten. The ego dies, but our triumphs over it remain, now and always. If we believe this, then everyone here knows just how much of Michael remains. Thank you for coming today, and may each of us find that peace. " And with that, she blew out her candle just when the sunlight returned.

"I saw him too." Thea whispered. She sat with Leveigh on the edge of the bed, and Oni leaning up against the far wall.

"Yes," Oni replied. "I'm not doubting my own perception, but what to make of it... A man in sunglasses, trench coat and a baseball cap, sitting in the pews, lighting a cigar instead of a candle in the middle of my eulogy, and smoking it. Did either of you recognize him?"

Leveigh and Thea shook their heads. The former replied, "So what are we thinking here? Machiavellian... Maybe a Ravenous operative? Or just some asshole with a problem?"

Thea shook her head. "The last option is dubious. Everyone in attendance should have had their credentials carefully vetted. If the man wasn't someone with a provable and important association to Michael, he took great pains to make it inside undetected."

Leveigh looked over to the bedroom window. "Hey... guys." He stood up, walking over. "Do you see this?"

They walked over. Etched into the glass along the highest right-side pane was a QR box alongside the scratchy likeness of a cigar.

Oni held her hand to the pane. "This was carved recently. There are still filaments of glass flaked on the grid... On the inside." She pressed her palm against the QR code. A red light flashed in the indent between her thumb and pointer finger, expanding as a line to her pinky as she held her hand phone-like to her ear and mouth.

"Good evening Captain." a voice growled through the call.

Oni replied calmly. "To whom am I speaking, and what do you want?"

"Come to the roof of the Hotel de Prague." the mysterious voice beckoned, "Only the three of you; no flight suits, no funny business— or many innocents will die. See you soon."

Oni turned to face her companions. "We have to go."

By the time they arrived, the sun was setting on the western horizon. The man who had disrupted Michael's funeral sat along the building's ledge—a polished green apple in the grasp of his right hand, acc- ompanied by a cigar lodged between the two upper fingers and balanced off the crest of the fruit.

He exhaled a stack of smoke, smiled, then palmed a quick bite.

"We did as you said," Oni called.

"We just want to talk. Who are you?"

The man pushed his trench-coat aside, revealing a raven emblem across his chest and an exquisitely long-barrel revolver holstered at the waist.

"You can call me 'Bow.'" he answered.

Oni felt a tremor in her chest. "Yes," she said flatly. "We've been introduced." Leveigh and Thea looked at her quizzically as Bow laughed.

"Well, not directly," he said. "Glad you recognized my signature though."

Thea's eyes narrowed, and her arms trembled as she stared at Bow. "This... *fuck* is the one who shot you?"

Bow wagged his finger. "Now, now. Don't get too agitated miss. I could kill all three of you before you so much as took a step, so I'd advise you to stay right where you are."

Oni stepped forward. "Threaten her again and the laser targeting you from high orbit will do to you what you failed to do to me."

Bow sighed. "You know, I tried to be a man of my word. I told you no funny business. I have this fuse," he said, showing a trigger button in his left hand. "But if I blow up the preschool across the street, I hardly think you'd be willing to listen to me, and what I've come to tell you is important. So shall we just agree to behave then?"

All was as tense a silence as death itself.

Thea was the first to speak. "How can we trust that what you tell us is true?"

Bow reached over and snagged a portfolio casing. "No need to take it from me." he exclaimed, tossing the bundle to K10 Theta. "This dossier has all the data you need to verify what I'm telling you independently. Some of the claims… You'll have to do some extra legwork to be sure, certainly. But there's enough in there to make my case."

Leveigh ran his hand through his hair with a sigh. "Okay," he said. "Tell us what you're here to tell us, and then let's be done."

Bow turned to face the sunset. "What if I told you that key politicians within your government have initiated a secret research program designed to engineer the structure of the Ethocracy into an autocratic society; that these leaders intend to decisively and effectively commandeer all apparatuses of the State for their own empowerment to such effect that they will be for all intents and purposes as immortal god-kings to the rest of us."

K10 Theta all exchanged sideways glances. "I confess," replied Oni, "that I am unsure if I even have the capacity to entertain such a notion." she frowned before continuing, "But I will try—what sort of research?"

Bow continued. "Weaponry that makes the technology of the Vanguard obsolete. Human clone farms made to harvest the blood of brainless infants as a component of a synthetic and intravenously administered anti-aging serum."

"Advancements in mind control and cloaking technology. Cybernetic stimulant enhancement systems for both physical and neurological amplification, and new types of suit technology designed for wet work and supremacy instead of guardianship. For starters."

"And because of the way in which they've controlled the information, only these leaders know anything about the workings of these pernicious developments. We cracked the most secure known data store in all the world and all we got, buried under layer after layer of encryption, were several breadcrumbs. Whoever is the architect of this work—they are *obsessively* careful."

He took a long drag of his cigar. On release, he continued. "Contained in the documents I've given you are the new methodologies by which we were able to crack your quantum encryptions, geospatial-logged screen capture of the activity of our operatives when they breached the server from the Archives with reference to a hidden cache for independent verification, and the deciphered information which corroborates my claims."

Leveigh picked up the dossier. "Suppose we do decide to believe what you're saying," he called. "Why are you telling us this?"

Bow stood up on the ledge of the belvedere, "because we want the same thing. You may be the ones in power, and we the opposition, but everyone on this rooftop wants to prevent this."

"You, to save the integrity of the government in which you believe, and I, to prevent the total domination of this perverted world order. Look at the dossier, and then decide where your priorities lie," The Ravenous said, then leapt off the edge of the building.

And they followed him to rooftop's limit, but when they looked over, he was gone.

"It turns out that 'knowing' something is a fiendishly elusive goal if what is hoped for is knowledge of an object for-itself. For its antecedent? Surely this is manageable. For its consequent? Absolutely. But the thing-for-itself evades the reach of our faculties of language, viz. the Understanding. We get our first whiff of this problem in Kant, a taste of it in Hegel and Wittgenstein, maybe some texture from Foucault's Archaeology; but until it is fully internalized, metabolized, and synthesized: we will continue to operate in error regarding the signification of our own life-world."

— Edgar von Galen, *In and For*

Chapter Twelve

§XIIA

"You're insane." Leveigh deadpanned. The three members of K10 Theta sat in Oni's cabin aboard the Aeschylus.

The walls were fashioned to be a virtual bulletin on which they had scattered media of various sorts displayed in a complex thought web. Thea sat on the edge of Oni's desk, while Oni chose to lay her back against the ground adjacent the window-bed, her feet propped up on the mattress and her head tucked in the cradle of her arms above it.

Thea shrugged. "You have a better idea of how to tackle this?"

Leveigh laughed nervously. "Than illegally breaching the Prometheus just to prove this conspiracy? We already have serious evidence. Let's just present it to High Command and let them sort it out. Why risk it? Why risk losing everything for this?"

Oni demurred, "Why be a Vanguard if you wouldn't? I thought the whole point of what we do is to follow what's right, no matter the personal cost."

The Corporal rolled his eyes. "Please don't rope me into your all-or-nothing moralisms Oni. I have the utmost respect for you, but I have the right to pursue a good life."

"We don't have to sacrifice ourselves on the word of some murderous lunatic just because he presents us with—"

Oni interjected, sitting up. "With what, Leveigh? Air-tight evidence? Documentation on massive research projects the Machiavellians couldn't dream of funding, research which, mind you, is predicated on scientific developments and resources to which they have absolutely no access? You know what's really insane? That we didn't see this sooner."

"If Michael hadn't been killed by that timed-EMP weapon, he'd have sniffed this out immediately. No way the Machiavellians can deploy this kind of innovation on that scale. It was a false flag operation for these traitors to test their ability to fight us should a war break out. Lucky for them they killed the only Vanguard who would have seen through their shit."

Leveigh sighed defeatedly. "Look… We don't know that's true. I understand why you're suspicious. I want to find out more too, but this isn't the way…"

"Actually," Thea countered, "we do know it's true." She walked over to one of the documents projected on the wall of the cabin. With the pull of her pointer fingers, she expanded it. "Meta-analysis of Senator McKinley's tech shows that he processed computations consistent with the developments in ballistic technology implemented in these weapons over six months ago."

"And, on the morning he was kidnapped, he made a file transfer to a MAC address also tied to hacking attempts made on the day of the Battle for Metropolis. We breached his device while you were investigating the dossier's proposed leads on which other Senators might be implicated."

Oni stepped in once more, this time as with an olive branch. "You remember how Michael reacted to McKinley's story… That's what pushed us to check. I know it's a lot, but it's the truth, whether or not you're ready for it. I'm sorry."

Leveigh ran his fingers through his hair. "Fffffuck," he mumbled. "I have two other Senators implicated on that front, by the way. Senators Watkins and Strauss. I'm running probability simulations now to narrow down prospects for the other two agents… It's not like I don't believe this is happening…"

"And I understand why it's risky to go to High Command when we don't know who else might be involved yet… I'm just scared shitless about doing what you're proposing we do to confront it."

Oni turned to look Leveigh in the eyes. "You know what needs to be done in order for us to move about the Prometheus undetected?" Leveigh nodded.

"Good. Then let's take the time we need to prep, and then do what needs to be done. This is bigger than us."

The newly-donned spray paint marbled the dim light of distant stars on each of their suits, which were now a dark grey and thoroughly iridescent. Strapped to their backs were tall, heavy black polyester bags with holstered equipment along the sides.

K10 Theta drifted along the proximity of the Prometheus behind a transport ship—hastily rigged with carbon sheeting—as it floated gently perpendicular to the megastructure.

Leveigh's voice chirped in over the Porta-COM "I'll deploy the oxygenated thermal flare to the Prometheus' local sensor when we're in range. Does everyone remember the plan?"

Oni and Thea nodded, to which Leveigh replied, "you guys ready to do this? If we make a single mistake, we're done for..."

Oni put a hand on Leveigh's shoulder sympathetically. "If we don't board the Prometheus now, we'll never forgive ourselves if it turns out we're too late to stop whatever they're planning. I hear your worry, but we have no choice." she replied. "Thea, ready the confabulation tech."

"Yes Captain," said Thea, as each of them haltered the backing of their respective guns along their shoulders.

"Three... Two... One... Begin boarding." The first to fire was Leveigh: he shot a thin missile into the broad side of the Prometheus. Once it made contact, the flare off the back of it ignited in a bright, brilliant blaze.

"Reposition." Oni called out, and they emerged in quick order from out of the cover of the transport. "Thea, you're up. Let's make this quick." Thea and Oni shot in quick succession. The first projectile to land on the hull was a metal ball with red diodes, stuck to the glass plating with a thick, clear gelatin.

The glass rippled, and when Oni's shot came through—another ball with blue diodes—it pressed effortlessly through the glass on-board the Prometheus. "Grab on tight." she said. Thea and Leveigh huddled close, and then with the flick of a switch on her device, K10 Theta rappelled through the glass and into the living quarters on-deck.

"Now." Oni ordered. Leveigh pulled a fuse from his person and pressed the button.

The lights went out, and all was darkness for a moment until a green light took its place. A voice came on the intercom,*"This is an official announcement from the Regulatory Committee aboard the Prometheus. Code green. We are investigating the source of a power disruption and will provide information and instructions as necessary. In the interim, please find your way to any small pressurized compartment to help reduce stress on the Auxiliary system. Thank you."*

The room was standard for Senator living quarters—rather less spartan than the Vanguard equivalent; this one furnished in a modernist Viennese style. The vague scent of essential oils permeated the cabin.

"Alright K10, you know the drill," Oni began. "Let's get down to tech storage and find the devices which were requisitioned for the research in question." They changed out of their suits, underneath which was standard casual dress.

Refitting their backpacks, Oni continued, "Everyone equipped to probe their respective items?" she asked. "Fair warning—If the answer's no we might have a problem."

K10 Theta fanned out of the quarters and into the main channel corridor for Section J4 of the Prometheus. Traffic was sparse. Several minutes into their excursion, a slender man in Senator's garb with a scar across his mouth and cheek waved down Thea.

"Hey, good to have a Vanguard on-board!" he called, half between a whisper and a yell. "Any idea what's going on here? Only been Elect for a year but this is the first outage we've had since then. I know we have full Auxiliary, but it's still unsettling you know?"

Oni and Leveigh kept walking. Thea met her interlocutor close. "Hi there! Yeah I understand where you're coming from. Can't say I have an idea as of yet. I was just heading to Regulatory station to go ask about it and see if some assistance might be necessary. You have a QR designation I could snag? I'd be glad to give you a call when I know more."

The Senator shook his head. "No, no worries, I'm sure you're plenty busy, just as I'm sure that this will all resolve itself soon. Thanks for your service!" he waved, nodding with a friendly comportment as he walked past.

By the time Thea caught up with the other two, they'd made it to the central hub. Ident-fixtures littered the entrances that dotted the grand hall corridor.

"It was a stupid risk." Leveigh whispered, scoldingly.

Thea shrugged. "He's the one who called me over. Had to act natural. We still haven't given any tangible sign of our presence on-board. We've disabled the tracking on our suits and ship, security feeds are down... By the time they know what's happened, if they figure it out, we'll have all the physical evidence we need to indict them. Relax. We're good."

Leveigh nodded. "Yeah... I think nerves are still getting the best of me. Sorry." While they spoke, Oni jogged ahead, slipping a glove onto her hand before placing it on the Ident-fixture.

The IDF's AI chimed in, "*Due to the inaccessibility of security feeds, more verification is necessary. Please remit finger for blood sample or wait for termination of code green. We apologize for the inconvenience.*"

Oni palmed a small device from the side pocket of her backpack. It snapped onto the face of the IDF magnetically. The AI intoned once more, "*sample completed. Thank you,*" and the door opened.

They walked into the tech storage facility. But, when they rounded the corner into the main equipment cache to begin their work, they were met by seven suited Vanguards.

"K10 Theta, you are remanded into T6 Alpha's custody under the command of Colonel Malweise Baker for attempted espionage on the Prometheus, and conspiracy with a Ravenous operative and known enemy of the state. Take off your backpacks, turn around and be prepared to board a transport vessel for egress to a secure facility for questioning."

Malweise stepped up to confront them. "Captain Anagonye: you fought with great courage in the battle for Metropolis. It is a shame to see you've decided to take a different path."

Oni blinked. "Malweise Baker…" she started, turning her head. "You were the ranking officer in that affair, if I recall."

Malweise nodded. "Yes, that is correct. I'm also the one who submitted the recommendation for your promotion to High Command."

"It's interesting," Oni pondered, "you explicitly stated to High Command before reinforcements arrived that, and I quote, 'they appear to have no equipment which may pose a threat to our forces.' A strange caveat to an ordinary ground report. As a result, none of our transport ships engaged in stealth or counter-attack maneuvering to land, prioritizing haste over safety." She blinked once more. "What do you think about that, Flight Officer Beckett?"

Thea stepped forward. "I think it's strange ma'am. I think it's an awful coincidence that the same officer would be here now to intercept us too, considering the contents of our investigation."

Malweise's gaze narrowed. "I'd be careful, Captain. Wouldn't want to make any more enemies today if I were you."

The Colonel stepped past them, gesturing. "Alright, let's clear out of here." Lead by the T6 squadron; Oni, Thea, and Leveigh were escorted out into the grand hall. When they came forth, a deep pulse of sound breached the full length of the cabin, and emergency flood lights filled the perimeter. A figure stepped out from behind the doorway to the flight hall.

Oni squinted. "Corvin? Is that you?" she called out hopefully. But, there was no reply.

The ships intelligence chimed in once more. "*Grand Hall Auxiliary systems compromised. Venting emergency oxygen to maintain cabin pressure.*"

Great streams of gas spurted out from the support beams along each wall. As the man stepped forward into the light, Oni's heart sank. The towering figure wore dense-plated armor, opal-hued and lustrous in its finish. He donned a sleek, jet black cloak and cowl, and a visor which seemed fashioned from the design of a vanguard flight-suit, but clouded so as to give no view of the face of its wearer. Strapped behind his head was the bulky cross-guard of a sword.

"Welcome, Colonel." A mechanically-distorted voice called out. "I see you got my message, but… there has been a mistake. I'm afraid I must ask you to stand aside," the figure explained, pulling out his sword in a flourish.

The blade behaved strangely. The body of the weapon was distorted, as if one examined the length of it through a haphazardly-framed kaleidoscope. Steel-blue light seemed to arc and discharge from each shard, all of which was bound up in a field of blurring and uncertainty, the individual fragments vibrating and shifting in sudden bursts.

The noise of the weapon was something between a constant strand of thunder and a jet-engine cutting through the sky, and the weapon's incandescent light glinted off the sheen of the armor, making clear the sigil of a raven in-flight.

Oni turned her head. "We need our flight suits," she spoke plainly, but Malweise ignored her—instead addressing his attention to the Ravenous.

A member of T6 Alpha called out, "Ravenous Thane: Lower your weapon, and we will not harm you. You have five seconds to comply." He ordered. A moment passed, and then T6 began to meet the Ravenous' pace, closing the distance between them.

What happened next was a dizzying progression of blood and violence. The Ravenous Thane plunged his blade into the chest of the first Vanguard to reach him, seamlessly weaving it out of the combatant and through the torso of the one adjacent. With his left hand, he grasped the visor of a third Vanguard and collapsed its structural integrity into the skull of its wearer in a dull eruption of cranial viscera.

He then slammed his sword through the abdomen of the last opponent, planting them into the wall. Stretching his neck as he flexed gently, Thane walked towards the remaining members of T6 Alpha, who arrested their advance immediately. "How…" the furthest of them gasped.

"It is all the same to me," Thane grimaced, "that Prometheus shall be christened with the blood of the pretenders." As he closed the gap between them, he reached a gauntlet back towards the sword. A red light coursed through it, quickly matched by with the same in the cross-guard of his sword before the weapon ripped out of the wall and flew back into his hand.

K10 Theta moved to exit towards J4, but Malweise yelled out, "Vanguards, do not allow Oni Anagonye and her conspirators to flee: we cannot allow their treachery to go unanswered. Block their exit. I will handle this." They complied, guarding the portal to the J4 corridor.

"An honorable man. How refreshing." Thane called out. He planted the blade in the floor. "We will settle this in the way of our ancestors." the Ravenous explained, twirling his cape to rest upon the cross-guard of his weapon. His arms barred out, ready for manual combat.

The Colonel stepped forward. "I don't know about all that," he answered flatly, walking towards his adversary. "But I will make you answer for what you've done. These were my people you slaughtered. You never said— "

Thane tilted his head. "Computer," he said, "cease strength augmentation protocol."

Malweise's footing loosened. "Are… Are you surrendering?" he stammered.

"I am what you can make of me, Colonel." said the Ravenous Thane "If I am your possession, then show me your claim. But I warn you— if you move to strike me, then your life shall depend on whether your suit can fill the chasm between our Wills; for I am a force of nature, and you are no yeoman." And with that, Thane's guard lowered. He folded his arms behind his back.

The first two punches thrown by Colonel Baker, aimed towards the Ravenous' visor, were swiftly evaded. At the third punch, to which Malweise strongly committed, the Ravenous Thane buckled his torso swiftly. The Colonel stumbled into Thane's shoulder along his own center of gravity, and fell head-first onto the ground. The Thane turned gently, bringing his arms forward.

"What a shame," his modulated voice breathed, "I had hoped you'd be surprising." Thane leapt upon the Colonel as he struggled to regain footing, wrapping his arms and torso with his legs as he struck Malweise Baker's visor with stunning force, over and over again.

Oni looked urgently towards K10's keepers. "Please… None of this is what it seems. Let us help you. I am Captain Oni Anagonye. We are your friends."

T6 Alpha's remaining members looked at one another. One spoke up. "You're staying here. If you want us to trust you, let us help Colonel Baker without fleeing. Your innocence and his culpability can be determined in arbitration." Thea and Leveigh nodded with unease, the three of them moving aside for the remainder of T6 squadron to protect their leader.

As soon as they moved towards the Ravenous, Thane resumed augmentation—vaulting off the Colonel and somersaulting towards his sword. He grasped his cloak and threw it hastily at Malweise before wrenching the blade from rest. Activating the aeronautics of his flight suit, he sailed lethally into the next of three combatants. Oni could see the energy shield falter along the longitude of the blade's thrust as it carved into the Vanguard's breast and up through the side of the neck.

The second Vanguard rocketed towards the Ravenous, but was deflected by Thane's own shielding, rebounding in the air. Thane glanced at Malweise before leaping towards his assailant, grabbing the airborne Vanguard by the neck and throwing her into the Colonel just as he found his footing.

Readjusting his grip on the blade, the Ravenous Thane leaned his weight into the weapon, plummeting its mass to skewer them one into the other. Without a second's delay, he reactivated the jet tech of his suit, closing the distance between him and the last T6 Vanguard, shouldering the survivor into the wall before plunging his fist clear through the suit and into the chest. Blood spurted out of the gap in the suit's plating.

The Ravenous stared with voracious intensity as he rammed the critically-injured Vanguard into the wall behind him. Pinning his victim there, Thane wrestled him into the middle of the nearest gaseous jet-stream.

"Are you afraid?" he queried, clawing his open palm through the glass of the Vanguard's visor, he tore off the helmet to reveal the expression of unmitigated terror. "Did you imagine that out this dream would float a cloud of riches?" The Vanguard reached helplessly for relief.

"Oh, what men might give to dream again." The Ravenous growled. Lifting the Vanguard above his head, Thane whirled, slamming the side of his victim's face straight into the floor. With a crack, the last of T6 Alpha crumbled, motionless, and lay without volition ever after.

K10 Theta did not wait to see these last moments unfold. As the Ravenous reveled in his cruel exposition, they fled.

§XIID

"I don't understand," Leveigh muttered. "He could have prioritized us easily. None of the Vanguards were actually a threat to him."

K10 Theta sat in the transport, earthward bound. The weight of the silence was powerful inertia to the expression of thoughts which abounded.

Thea shook her head. "I don't think it was his intention to stop us."

Oni and Leveigh turned their heads as she continued. "Think about it... From the government's perspective, we were committing espionage. Vanguards intercepted our efforts, but as far as any onlookers are concerned—we were freed by an elite Machiavellian warrior with previously-unseen technology."

"That, and apparently the government knew about our meeting with Bow. As far as anyone watching is concerned, we're not just seditious; we're major players working against the health of the Ethocratic state…"

Thea looked out the front of the shuttle, soaking in the sheen of mother Earth on their approach.

"We need to go somewhere no one can find us." She continued.

Oni nodded. "Computer, navigate us to a remote location within 1000km of Metropolis with low altitudinal visibility."

The computer replied, "*Location found. Commencing landing sequence.*"

"Okay," said Oni, "we'll lay low. But I know you Thea—you have an instinct here that you're not sharing. What are you thinking?"

Thea held her hand in her head. "As far as I can tell, only two possibilities remain. The Machiavellians are orchestrating dissent within our government in order to weaken it. Either this is a genuine effort to dismantle a system they correctly perceived as corrupt or; —"

Leveigh leaned forward. "Or?"

Thea turned to face them. "Or, they already have a hold on our government, and this move of ours was exactly what they had hoped for."

"And now," Oni added, "they've succeeded in discrediting the evidence against them 'ere we could even wield it. They've won. They weaponized the truth in order to conceal their lies, and it seems like they've gotten away with it."

"So how do we get back at them?" asked Leveigh.

The shuttle burned with intense red brightness as it broached the atmosphere. The glint of it reflected brightly off the dark of Oni's stare. "We give them hell." she replied, and from there the raucous trembling of the cabin filled all space for discourse.

"My wife died very suddenly from an embolism in our late thirties, shortly after she gave birth to our firstborn. For years after that, all I could think about was how desperately I wished that we had shared just one last intentional, sweet, and affectionate moment before she passed. But the expanse of a person's life lived out in-full provides a wide perspective, and in my twilight years I realize that I would have always longed for one more, just one more, in an infinite series of unrequited dreams. And on that realization, I remembered that it was my dreams for which she first fell in love with me, as I in her—by making new ones, I honored an important part of what we had shared. Through this I learned that although serenity is peace, it is also renewal."

— Edgar von Galen in interview, reflecting on his life

Chapter Thirteen

§XIIIA

The rocky southern coast of Croatia was painted with the orange light of the evening sun, which hung from delicate clouds woven as a tapestry of coral, fuchsia, and all imaginable gradients thereof.

The indigo waves lapped along the pebble shore, fizzing through sand and sediment before rolling back into the deep. A fusion of the ocean water and flora aromated the open air. Pollocked along the crevice of the bay were blurred brushstrokes of lilac and evergreen intermingled with the leafy, low-hung branches of the sparse arboreality.

Tucked close to the base of the cliff—facing some eighty meters from the water was a shell of a house, built from stone and wood—no doors or windows remained, and the roof was a thin smattering of logs. The flora had long-since overtaken the structure, and although in any meaningful sense the house had been abandoned, the view this fact arose in the coastline was a prepossessing sight.

Nestled on the ridge-line was the Vanguard transport ship, underneath which were the members of K10 Theta sitting around a makeshift fire made of driftwood and brush.

"Hey Leveigh," said Oni, "Did you handle our personnel ships? I totally forgot."

Leveigh nodded. "I had them autonomously stationed beneath an abandoned underpass on the outskirts of Metropolis before we even started, and directed them en-route as soon as we landed here. They should be along at any minute."

"Thanks." Oni answered faintly. She blinked. "That sword. What was that? It just—completely ignored the energy shielding tech, and it looked like it cut through the flightsuits as though they were butter too. That's supposed to be impossible."

Leveigh nodded. "I read a bit about them in the dossier. They're called 'Quantic blade tech'. Essentially, they're a workaround to our system's way of measuring the velocity of mass by putting the specialized matter into an excited and 'uncertain' state.'"

"The phenomenon requires tremendous energy, so the material effuses an electrified plasmatic substance as part of the cooling system of the design. It's ingenious. And it completely negates most of our tangible advantages over the Machiavellians."

"Fortunately for us, it also costs a fortune to produce, so I think we needn't worry about mass adoption among the rank-and-file."

An ember cracked in the fire pit. "So," said Thea, after a sober silence, "what are we thinking here? 'Cause I've been going through every option I can conjure and nothing helpful seems to be coming up so far. Anyone?"

Oni and Leveigh shook their heads.

"Right," Thea soured, "so we're fucked, basically."

Oni rubbed her face, then anxiously played with her hair. "No, not fucked… just stumped. I think? I don't know… guys, there's something you should know… Something big."

Thea and Leveigh glanced at one another. The latter spoke up, "Okay, well… you know you can tell us anything. What is it?"

"No," said Oni, shaking her head. "This isn't something I can just tell you. You have to see it all for yourself I think, or you won't believe me. It's too much to believe from words alone… Computer, project all recordings related to the person Corvin Elrick Ratzinger."

The AI piped up, *"starting holographic projection."* And then K10 Theta witnessed all that Oni had seen of the All-Father. When they were finished, Oni spoke up once more.

"I also chronicled a dream in my diary in which he quite literally visited me. You can read it yourself if you'd like," she offered, tossing a leather journal into Thea's splayed arms. The word 'Phenomenology' was printed across it in burned, brilliant letters. "Page four hundred and thirty nine, for quick reference."

"Oni," Thea whispered, stunned. "I don't understand. Why haven't you told us about this before now? Told me? Told anyone?"

Oni's brow furled. "I've been scared out of my mind. Every time I see him, it's like I bleed out of the reality in which we live and into some strange Otherworld—where I don't know the rules, the choices I have aren't clear to me, all with consequences that I didn't even know were possible… maybe some which I can scarcely even imagine as of yet. I didn't know how you two would react, and that scared me." Thea nodded, though her shoulders were hunched.

"The man who moved us to Prague after the fight with Claw," she said quietly. "that was him. That was Corvin, Leveigh. Right?"

The Corporal nodded, and a moment passed to let the revelations sink in.

"So," said Leveigh breaking the quiet, "Are you going to do it then? Become… ascendant? Damn, what a strange thing to ask."

Oni shook her head. "I don't know. I was hoping we could talk about that. I trust you two more than anyone else in the world. You are brilliant, insightful, and tenacious. Between the three of us, can we come up with any other plausible solution for how to approach this Machiavellian coup?"

There was none but the sound of silence among them. "Okay," Oni sighed. "We're all tired. It's been a long day. I suppose—" she said, but her attention wandered as she caught sight of the personnel ships landing along the shore line.

As they began to settle, she resumed. "I suppose we better eat, rest, maybe enjoy the water a little. It'll be a long time again before we get another good opportunity to sleep under the blanket of a clear night sky."

§XIIIB

And so they ate and rested for a time. Leveigh was the first to wander off into the abandoned house, a sleeping bag and pillow in-hand. Oni and Thea sat on the shoreline, looking at the stars and how they glistened off the surface of the waters.

"It doesn't make sense." said Oni.

"Hmm?" hummed Thea. Oni turned her head gently.

"Why is Corvin offering this to me? Surely there are better prospects somewhere in the world... Someone. Anyone really."

Thea raised an eyebrow. "You know, for a genius, you're really quite thick sometimes. If you can't see why Corvin would choose you, then you're either too modest or need a therapist hun, because you're incredible."

"Besides," she speculated, "based on the way he worded it, this doesn't sound like some prize that can be bestowed. It's more like a latent potential to be unlocked. Some people are double-jointed or have webbed toes... I guess you have this...? Weird shit happens, but what are you gonna do about it?"

Oni laughed, "while I in principle understand your point; on behalf of the double-jointed and webbed-toe communities, I feel obliged to register some displeasure. But yeah, that was the sense I got from it too—the bit about unlocking some sort of untapped capacity in me. It's just weird to think about, you know?"

Thea nodded her head slowly, then shook it. "Nope. Can't say I do. Sorry." she said with a grin. "Oh, and if you ever go through something heavy like this again and neglect to even let me know you're struggling, I'm going to sass you all the way to Saturn. Understood?"

Oni smirked back, rubbing the second-least left-side finger as she replied, "Yes, love. Though in truth it will be a relief; At least then I'll be in proximity to some sort of ring."

Thea's eyes bulged. "Oh you did not just go there," she barked under the pale blue dusk. "YOU DID NOT JUST GO THE—HEY GET OVER HERE!" she yelled, tackling Oni into the water.

Oni grappled herself on top of her lover and stuck out her tongue before gleaming with a full-toothed smile. "I love you." said Oni tenderly.

Thea soaked in every detail of the moment. "I love you too." she whispered, displaying her affection with a long and tender kiss.

A stiff sadness came over Thea's face after a moment. "Oni, if you accept Corvin's offer... Will we still be able to be together?"

Oni pressed her face against Thea's cheek. "Nothing could ever keep us apart."

§XIII§

"God damn it!" Leveigh's voice called out from the beachside. "No, no, no, —Fuck!" Oni and Thea fluttered out to meet their colleague, who was pacing back and forth, his fingers padding the back of his head. His gear lay at his side, and his computer tablet rested on the ground beside it.

"Hey, Corporal," called Thea worriedly. "you okay?"

Oni caught up quickly. "Yeah, what's got you unsettled?"

Leveigh was shaking. "It's over. We've lost."

Oni shook her head. "You can't be thinking like that Vanguard, we need you. What's got you saying this?"

Corporal Simoneau turned to face her. "It's gone. The data. Everything from the dossier. They breached my cybersecurity and erased every shred of it. It's the same computer MAC address we keep seeing... And that's not all..."

"I tried to access the backup I made at base, and it looks like our connection to the Aeschylus network has been terminated. High Command must have locked us out. We're officially fugitives. Public enemies. Personae non grata." he said defeatedly, grabbing the tablet and sitting into the nook of his backpack.

"I don't understand," said Thea, "reducing our clearance to general public access would make sense, but I'm sure that High Command still wants to communicate with us. What about your access isn't working? Is the system refusing to authenticate your credentialing or is it something else?"

Leveigh shook his head vigorously, "No, no, nothing like that. The tablet isn't even picking up a signal from the Aeschylus; it's like our tech has a blind spot for it now or something. I still have access to the general ground-level public feed though…"

Oni's eye wandered the skyline. "It's obvious what we have to do now, isn't it?" She turned to face K10 Theta. "Corvin also has the data from the Archives. He's our last chance."

Thea's expression sank. "You want to partner with him? I don't know if I'm—" she hesitated. "I don't know if that's a good idea."

"Love," Oni cautioned, "We don't have a choice. Either we just leave the public to take our word for it, or we go to him, and make it available for everyone to see for themselves. This must have been why he stole the data. He knew that we'd find ourselves in this situation."

"Or," Leveigh added, still distracted by the screen of his tablet, "he just couldn't afford to rely on our efforts if we failed. Which, if that's the case… good on him." Leveigh's brow clenched tight. "Wait, what? Guys, this is weird…"

Oni faced away, stretching her arms. "I know. This is a lot to process and I know even Corvin's existence turns a lot of what we thought we knew on its head. I—"

"No," Leveigh interjected, "sorry, that's not what I meant. Look at this." he said, pointing to his screen. They obliged, but the screen seemed blank other than a 'live recording' interface.

"What are we looking at?" said Oni.

Leveigh looked up at her. "That is a live video feed for the Aeschylus. The one used by the World Interplanetary Initiative's Museum for the Public Understanding of Astronomy."

Thea shook her head. "I've been to that museum. They use Porta-COM tech to transmit that image. Video feed disruption is literally impossible."

Oni could feel her heart in her throat. "It's not a disruption. Look closely."

The faint contours of the megastructure subtly came into view. Every light aboard the vessel was off, except that the faintest red hue could briefly be seen flashing before large sections of the Aeschylus' hull ignited in an explosion of cataclysmic force.

"Why do humans do the work of story? Pick apart every substance and ordering in the cosmos and you will find no answers. You must simply ask them, the ones who tell us their tales. The answers will each be different, and yet genuine. Prod deep enough, and you will hear only autobiography, neat and clean as a fingerprint. Not all truth has at its heart some universal principle."

"Only the most basic elements of existence align under our scrutiny so amicably, and even these require the exquisite apparatus of science to be rendered comprehensible in any meaningful sense. The scientist delights in answering questions about that which is in the world; the philosopher remains to answer the for of the matter."

— Edgar von Galen, *In and For*

Chapter Fourteen

§XIVA

K10 Theta closed the gap between them and the Aeschylus without delay. They each flew in their respective personnel ships, and behind them the larger transport vessel travelled in their wake—though rather sluggish, as the three Vanguards were rocketing towards the wreckage of their home at a breakneck pace.

Within sixty kilometers of the hull, the forest of debris came into full view. Millions of little bits; shards of glass, metal poles, parts and pieces, and—to the grief of K10 Theta—many ravaged bodies drifting into the void of space.

"Oh God," Thea breathed through the Porta-COM connection with her cooperatives.

Leveigh was the first to break the stone-dead silence which followed. "I'll make my way over to the K10 transport cargo sector since it seems to remain in-tact. See if I can't get these boats moving and receiving for any survivors."

"Good," Oni answered. "Thea and I will do what we can to get people moving in that direction. Heat signatures indicate a lot of activity still going on on-board. It looks like a combat operation… Leveigh, once you get that settled we may end up needing you our way."

"Copy that," said Leveigh, as he veered his ship to the K10 transport bay.

Thea began flying up and over to the stern-side portion of the Aeschylus. "I'll take the upper intact portion. Seems like there could be a lot of people there that could use help. Take care of yourself guys."

Oni flew to the lower section which remained in-tact. "Computer, eject me in alignment with the minor hull breach in sector Q5." The compartment's hydraulics activated, and she was gently relinquished towards a car-sized gap in the hull of the Aeschylus.

She emerged in a hallway adjoining the Sector Q conference theater. Oni could hear the commotion of gunshots and screams the moment she landed.

The intercom aboard the Aeschylus blared, *"Code red—critical damage to core systems detected. Evacuate immediately. Oxygen saturation at 23.5%. Three minutes to secure airflow."*

Moving hastily, Oni brought herself into the dim fire-filled light of the conflict. The auditorium was decimated—electrical fires littered the apparatus of the area and along the high portion of the wall— a gaping chasm into the open void sat aligned with our burning sun, patched by a wave of energy shielding.

A familiar, ominous voice filled the smokey air. "It is over Vanguards." called out the Ravenous Claw, "You have fought valiantly, but now, with your suits rendered useless, your ship a corpse drifting through space: it is time to relent and give penitence. The devout among you will be spared. Be of faith. Come to my feet and you shall be richly rewarded. As for the rest of you—" said the Ravenous, pausing briefly to snatch a wounded Vanguard from nearby rubble, "forever onwards shall you burn in the heart of Gehenna."

He tossed the injured Vanguard star-wards, corpsified on the edge of the damaged hull before plummeting into the beyond.

Oni emerged from the shadows. "You're right Claw. It is over. Just not for the Vanguard."

The mechanized warrior turned to face his adversary. "Oni Anagonye, back from the dead! This time, let's make sure it sticks. Boys, kill her."

All guns of a half-dozen Machiavellians turned on her. The hail of bullets fizzled out of the air in front of her uselessly.

"Well," demurred Claw, "looks like we've had a recent boarding. Lucky girl evaded our EMPs. That's okay. I will take care of her myself."

The next half-minute was a deadly game of tag. Oni vaulted, not at Claw, but at the first bundle of insurgents she could reach. Dispatching with them through a sequence of blows, she catapulted to a third, slamming his temples with a fist on either side.

All this had occurred before Claw could reach her, but when he swung in to get ahold of Oni, she ducked, grabbing the tactical rifle of the Machiavellian beside her on the floor and somersaulting underneath Claw's stance.

With a flourish, she righted herself before taking three quick shots to dispatch of the rest; the suit's visual and somatic targeting systems assisting with the quick work of securing the safety of her fellow Vanguards.

Claw laughed. "You think any of this matters? Your people are done for, they have no exit strategy. Hundreds of my soldiers roam along the remains of the Aeschylus. And after I kill Ms. Anagonye, the rest of you will die by my hand as the price of her insolence."

The intercom of the Aeschylus could be faintly heard in the space between them, once again affirming their dire circumstances. "*Code red—critical damage to core systems detected. Evacuate immediately. Oxygen saturation at 21%. Ninety seconds to secure airflow.*"

"You talk a big game," said Oni, stretching her arms and neck. "Let's see what you've got."

They collapsed on one another like particles in a chamber, the resulting tension cracking out with a grenadish bang exploding throughout the cabin. Immediately, Claw pincered Oni to the ground, swinging his adjacent arm up to collapse through Oni's exposed chest.

The Captain reacted instinctually, placing her arms above her head and blasting the ground behind her. The first expulsion shot them upwards off the ground, and the second battered Claw into the rubble.

Pounding into the mechanical armor in a fury of arcing punches, Oni eviscerated the casing of Claw's haphazard suit. Slowing down to hone in on a sequence of terrific, pounding strikes—Oni spoke tersely between the lunges.

"You thought that just because you beat me when I was concussed, with the cowardly help of a sharpshooter, that you were somehow my better?" she seethed. The hydraulic machinations of the suit were wrested, and Claw sat motionless in the heap of cement and metal. Oni stepped down from the remains of the mechanized suit, turning to face the Vanguards who were all in various states of dishevelment; watching the scene in disbelief.

The intercom alerted the crew of the Aeschylus once more. *"Code red —critical damage to systems detected. Evacuate immediately. Oxygen saturation is now below the threshold of survivability. Please follow code protocols to secure safe egress. Thank you."*

Oni called out, bright as a morning ray, "alright Vanguards, take these weapons and make your way to the K-10 hanger for evacuation to Earth. Don't worry: your suit uses a passive oxygenation system, so the EMP won't affect your ability to breathe in this climate. Corporal Leveigh Simoneau has pre-programmed a drop point for us to reconvene on the planet."

"Now get down there, protect one another, and show them why we are the Vanguard. I will make sure the Ravenous operative is detained and then I will continue assisting with the evacuation of other quadrants. Be brave. The Ethocracy needs you."

§XIVB

The Vanguards hustled to follow this order, which fed Oni with renewed confidence as she turned to face Claw once more. "I am no fool," she said. "I know you can exit that suit, and that if I leave you here you will probably follow me until you have reinforcements. I can't let that happen, and the stakes are too high right now for me to hold back. If you don't emerge now, and peacefully, I will have to kill you. Do you understand?"

The framework of the suit unfolded, from which emerged a shadowy figure. His under-suit was also fashioned from Vanguard technology, yet he had made more significant modifications from Thane's design. The helmet was shaped to evoke the vague impression of a dragon or serpent, and the material of the suit itself was not like a flight-suit at all. Instead, heavy mail plates of a matted black covered him head to toe, and along each arm extended two mid-length Quantic blades on either end, paired with a shorter one midway along the hand, all of which came together to form a maleficent pair of claws.

"It's rather on the nose, isn't it?" Oni laughed. Claw ignored the banter, walking towards her at a brisk pace. Swing by swing, Oni dodged Claw's triad of lethality with swift evasive maneuvers. The Quantic tech buzzed through the air with each pass, and Oni could feel the heat emanate like the close pass of cinders billowing through the air adjacent her.

"Careful, those things are sharp." Oni cautioned, "someone might get hurt if you keep playing with them like that."

Another series of lunges thrown, only one of which forced Oni to resettle her footing, but then on the follow-through—Claw swung his leg out on Oni's kneecaps, and she tumbled. Rolling over, she caught his arms just in time. His right claw was safely extended out and over them, Oni controlling it at the wrist. The left, however, hovered inches parallel to her visor.

Holding his arm steady, sweat from the intense heat fogged up the lens of her face mask. Wheeling the Ravenous off her with a rocket-aided fling of the legs, she jetted away from him; pressing the switch in the nape of her shoulder to collapse the flightsuit's helmet into the fabric of its body armor. A respirator coiled around her head and mouth as she did so.

He closed the gap between them quickly, and after several more swipes at her, Oni went in for a punch. Claw ducked, and in that motion raked his claw against the outside of her thigh. She yelled, grasping at the wound.

"Oni are you alright?" Thea called out over the Porta-COM tech. Oni sought to settle herself enough to reply, but the pain was overbearing.

"Okay, no worries love." Flight Officer Beckett continued, "I'm on my way. Just take care of yourself until Leveigh and I get there. He said he was wrapping up a minute ago. I'll contact him now and we'll make our way over at once."

Claw's countenance manifest in the silhouette of his armor against the flame-light. His shoulders loosened as he walked towards his adversary. Oni's breath settled, and she stood, striking her arms into a defensive stance.

"It's over." the Ravenous menaced. "Surrender now, and your deaths will be swift."

"Not even close Claw." Oni heaved a blinkered sigh, hyping her breath for the fight ahead.

"If this is the best you got, then I'm still going to—"

"Oni." A voice called out on the edge of her vision. It was Leveigh, hands behind his back, knees on the ground as the Ravenous Thane rested his Quantic blade inches above the Vanguard's head.

"I'm sorry," Corporal Simoneau called out.

Captain Anagonye's breathing tightened, each repetition becoming more shallow and stiff.

Then, her lungs felt as though cut with glass as she saw Thea vault from the gape of the ship's hull down onto Claw, blasting him with a cone of white-hot fuel after pinning him to the ground. Oni called out to her love as the Ravenous screamed, muffling the sound of her voice enough that Officer Beckett did not register the predicament.

"THEA!" Oni cried, as she watched the long blade plunge into the chest of Leveigh Simoneau. The young Corporal collapsed as the Flight Officer stood off the agonized husk of the Ravenous Claw.

The Ravenous Thane charged at Oni and Thea as a rumble in the ship's engine core reverberated throughout the theater. Before they could react, the distance was closed—with three quick, swiping motions; Thea was cut down, Oni was ripped from shoulder to solar plexus, and her respirator was severed.

As she buckled in shock, the Ravenous Thane lifted his Quantic blade above Oni's head to plunge down through the whole of her.

But then she stood on the bright side of the moon, her injuries gone, and a familiar face at her side. "It's time." Corvin explained, placing his hand on her shoulder.

"I know." she replied, "I'm ready. Let me go."

Corvin shook his head. "No, not to die little one. It's time to live."

""If there were no eternal consciousness in a man, if at the bottom of everything there were only a wild ferment, a power that, twisting in dark passions, produced everything great or inconsequential; if an unfathomable, insatiable emptiness lay hidden beneath everything, what would life be but despair?"

— Soren Kierkegaard, *Fear and Trembling*

§XVA

Oni looked at her surroundings. "Okay, I know this is supposed to be a solemn moment, but I have to ask… any reason we're on the moon?"

Corvin grunted. "I've got business to attend to."

"…On the moon." Oni replied with the utmost incredulity, to which Corvin nodded in the affirmative. "Got it, just wanted to be clear, but I see there's no chance of that happening. How've you been?"

Corvin grinned. "I've been… occupied. Supporting your efforts from behind the scenes, Captain." he said with a playful salute. "How about you?"

Oni looked down at herself, padding at the sight where her wound had been. "I seemed to have been doing poorly… From the looks of it, in the past tense. Any chance you can help a sister out with an explanation or something?"

Corvin's lip pouted softly. "That depends; are you ready to embrace your destiny?"

The quietude of space was a strange juxtaposition for the gravity of the moment, with a pale blue dot balancing the weight of the world which sat between them.

Oni blinked. "I'm not even sure what that means."

Corvin gestured at the hot white Sun. "take in the Light of the Eternal and claim for yourself the full potential of your Spirit."

Oni rested her hand on Corvin's shoulder. "You're going to have to help me a bit more than that, All-Father."

Corvin wheeled around, grasping Oni's forehead with the palm of his hand. Oni's vision ratcheted into an out-of-body perspective aboard the wreckage of the Aeschylus. She saw herself writhing for air, a tear streaming down her cheek as Thane brought his sword down on her: K10 Theta sprawled along the floor as the Ravenous stood victorious.

Forced into the perspective of her flightsuit's helm, she could hear herself calling out with weak cries. "Not again…. Please, I… let me breathe. I need— air. Please."

She snapped out of it, palming Corvin's hand from off her head. "HEY!" she yelled. "I DID NOT SAY THAT WAS WHAT I WANTED. Don't touch me again until I say you can. Do we have an understanding?"

Corvin nodded. "Sorry." he said, "I misunderstood. But this is what must happen in order for you to absorb the power of your full potential. May I continue? We've only just started and there's not exactly a wide window of opportunity to get this done."

Oni puffed her cheeks. "What if I say no?"

"You die." Corvin said flatly.

"Do I? That doesn't feel true."

Corvin began to pace restlessly. "Well… No, it's not entirely true."

Oni slanted her gaze with rich dubiousness. "I don't think this is one of those situations where partial accuracy is a thing."

"Okay," Corvin relented. "You wouldn't die. I'm sure you can already feel it in you now. You haven't wholly absorbed the gift of the Light, but some of it seeped into you the moment I laid my hands upon your head. That much cannot be helped."

Oni gazed at her own hands. She could feel her pulse seem to harmonize with a network of… ringing? Buzzing? Some brilliant shimmer of exuberance suffused her being, though the words seemed to be unconjurable. "So what does that make me? Not a god?"

"No," Corvin replied. "Not a god, but not fully mundane anymore either. Something in-between. There's a name for it—the ancients would call you dæmon."

Oni laughed. "You know, it's funny. My girlfriend is Japanese by ancestry. One of the first things she told me was that my name was very strange in her culture—that 'Oni' was akin to the word 'demon' in her native language. But in my culture, the name means something entirely different. It's something to the effect of "she who is prayed for", which is almost salvific in its connotation."

"Just as in the tension of my name between cultures, I now find myself treading the line between divinity and humanity with the moniker 'dæmon'? Serendipity is ever the strange bedfellow."

Corvin shrugged. "It worked for Socrates. I'm sure you'll find a way to make sense of it. Are you familiar with the concept of liminality?"

172

Oni shook her head.

Corvin nodded. "No worries. Essentially the idea is this—that in the rite of initiation, there is an intermediate phase: one no longer is possessed of the status they had before going in, but they still have yet to be confirmed into the symbolic form which the ritual is meant to bring about. The liminal phase of ritual is powerful but disorienting."

"Okay," said Oni. "So what are you saying?"

Corvin folded his arms. "I'm saying that we're playing a dangerous game. Take good care Oni Anagonye. I will see you again soon."

Oni began walking away from the All-Father, but paused, turning to face him. "You have the data from the Archives safe?"

Corvin nodded.

"See you soon," Oni replied, and with that, she was gone.

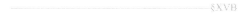

§XVB

The shards of the Quantic blade rattled in-place as Oni stood up, fingers outstretched as if to catch the weapon. As she rose, the flight suit tumbled off of her in pieces like dead leaves brushed aside the path of nimble feet. Beneath her under-suit, deep veins of cosmic, azure light radiated in gradual luminous cycles, while streams of like-energy pooled from her eyes as fog drifting in a gentle draft.

Thane staggered, pulling his weapon back with him. He rebounded, charging Oni full-tilt. Every swing of his blade was met with a finite plasmatic beam carved into reality, each of which disapparated whence his sword was rebounded. Then with a wave of her hand, the Ravenous Thane shot across the theater and into the far wall, the energy armor bracing him for impact. Still, he stumbled off of the force of the injury.

Oni turned her attention to the members of K10 Theta, lifting them with the gesture of her hands. White light filled the gape of their wounds, and when it dissipated, they were whole again. Then, with a turn of the palm, they disappeared.

As Thane regained his footing, Oni walked towards him. "I have witnessed your cruelty, Ravenous Thane." her voice rang out, but it was more than just hers alone—Oni spoke with all the voices of the millennia of Kindred spirit, "You will submit peacefully. One way or another, your bloodlust ends here."

When the Ravenous moved as if to strike her, she blasted him with a wave of energy, and he collapsed. "Remove your helmet, Thane. I want to see what the face of cruelty is with my own eyes."

The face shocked Oni into her ordinary countenance. "Heathrow?" she weeped, the light of her eyes quickly replaced with despair as the dæmon form subsided.

Senator Wilson unceremoniously boosted himself air-ward through the void of the Aeschylus' hull, uncollapsing his helmet as he rose. Oni shrunk to the ground, staring blankly forward as the wreckage of her home-life smoldered.

§XVC

"Why are we still here?" the voice of El spoke.

Corvin sat cross-legged in a basin of the bright side of the moon. "The peace of this place soothes me, calms my mind, and helps me get perspective."

"Perspective?" the apparition replied. "You're Omniscient. What more perspective do you need? We already have the essence of our purpose."

"See," Corvin said, hesitantly, "that's the thing. The trick of it all. Lumping 'understanding' and 'knowledge' together like they're interchangeable when they're not. As if awareness and choice could be collapsed into an unbudging atomism."

The shadow lingered, but did not reply. "I know you've sensed my hesitation." said Corvin. "You don't talk to me when I'm around her, and lately you have not spoken with me the way that you did when we first met."

El poured out into the space around him, plunging their surroundings into darkness. "Yes... I sense doubt in you where once there was faith. Do you no longer have the will to do what needs to be done?"

Corvin stood up. "Oh I know what needs to be done. I just don't think your way is right anymore. I'm not myself when I'm with you."

The shadow laughed. "Corvin, all yourself that is of any consequence is Ourself. There is no you without me, for we are All-Father. Do not forget this, lest you make an irrevocable mistake."

Corvin's eyes narrowed. "What you've just said... There is both truth and falsehood in it. Yes, we are both All-Father, but you are not grafted to the Light Eternal as I am, you are only Our afterimage. I should not even call you El anymore. Where once you were El, now you are merely Shadow. Your duplicity is laid bare, and it is only in the wake of me that you crawl upon the ground." A terrible gust passed them, moon dust kicking up all around.

"Oh, Corvin." the shadow sneered, "no being in the history of the world has fallen half so much as you in this moment. For in one fell swoop, you have doomed all life when a final solution was just within your reach."

The voice of El transformed into a dark and insidious tone, seeming to latch onto a different vocal origin. Nevertheless, as it contorted itself into the vastness of space, it proclaimed a parting thought.

"Your lack of wisdom has drained the world of its luster, and of all the places you could have chosen to take this stand, you picked the one location where darkness… might drift anywhere. Goodbye, All-Father. Know me now as a Darkness… Everlasting."

Corvin's face stayed motionless as the dust around him settled.

"It is impossible to escape the impression that people commonly use false standards of measurement — that they seek power, success and wealth for themselves and admire them in others, and that they underestimate what is of true value in life. And yet, in making any general judgement of this sort, we are in danger of forgetting how variegated the human world and its mental life are."

— Sigmund Freud, *Civilization and its Discontents*

Chapter Sixteen

§XVIA

The coffee wafted into his nostrils, folding on the stubble on his lip and cheeks before bracing his mind for the world.

This was the faintest of distinctions—as the office was a dream-like space wherein one might easily mistake themselves for the denizen of an otherworld: ferns spruced a futuristic architecture of sanded wood beams and wall-long light fixtures that suffused the air with warmth.

The beams themselves were carved out to make space for patterned rows of books. Ivy festooned the naked brick along the far wall, which was carved out by water which trickled down the surface ornamentally.

"How are you doing today, Mr. Kempf?" asked Leveigh.

Martin placed the coffee cup at his knees. "Not great. I'm not sleeping well, and I keep feeling overwhelmed. But there's peace sometimes too, and that is also new."

Leveigh nodded. "I'm sorry sleep has been elusive. Is it that you can't get comfortable and are not falling asleep, or do you find yourself waking up throughout the night?"

"Nightmares." Martin replied curtly.

"Do you want to talk about them?" said Leveigh. They sat for a moment while Leveigh took another sip from his cup, his fingers curling around its warmth from out of long sleeves that blanketed the length of his hands.

Martin pulled out a cigarette.

"Put that back, no smoking in here." Leveigh explained tersely, as Martin brandished his lighter. The patient rescinded his fix, looking back and forth across the room before he leaned back.

"So are you like a doctor or something? I feel like I've seen you on the news… or somewhere before." he asked.

Leveigh nodded. "You have. I'm a member of K10 Theta, a Vanguard who is currently being tried for high treason in Metropolis. I'm also a jew." he explained, looking intently into Martin's eyes. The latter shrugged.

"Might not want to advertise those things together. Could be my bias isn't as changed as you think, Mister…?" Martin inquired.

Leveigh shook his head. "Corporal Leveigh Simoneau. Or doctor, if you'd prefer. Most people don't. But both statements are true. I'm quite proud of them, actually."

Martin's head tilted.

"Well," Leveigh explicated, "I can trace my lineage to both Freud and Wiesel, so that's pretty wonderful… And I'm being prosecuted for efforts which were actually aimed at saving the Ethocracy. But we failed. Live and learn."

Kempf leaned forward. "Oh, you're a Vanguard? There's been no news to the public yet about whether or not any of you even survived. Jesus. What are you doing here with me?"

Leveigh pointed downwards. "Well, we have these neat little ankle bracelets that can knock us out from anywhere with the click of a button, and we're being actively monitored. Not much trouble I can get into. And although no one is holding me to it anymore, service is a cornerstone of Vanguard public life."

"So, here I am: a doctor in the philosophy of mind doing counseling things on his downtime. Enough about me though, I think. Let's get back to you." he said with a resigned smile, which belied his sadness.

Martin cleared his throat. "Where to begin?"

"I think it goes something like, 'a Nazi and a Jew walk into a therapy session.'" Leveigh laughed, then straightened up in his seat, pointing a finger at Martin sternly.

"I won't." Martin demurred uncomfortably.

"Good." Leveigh replied somewhat sardonically before side-eyeing him. "I'm watching you... So, are you going to talk to me, or are we going to sit here all day?"

Martin sat back, closed his eyes, and sighed. "My brother was always my guiding light in life. Mom and dad were abusive, both to their children and in their drug habits. Sometimes I'd go to school with burns and bruises on my arms. My teachers never gave a shit."

"But my brother would dress them every time, asking me how they happened, and apologizing as if he were their cause. He was ten years my elder, but it felt like he was my real parent. Like I was his. After he killed himself when I was sixteen, I was alone."

Leveigh's lower lip curled as his brow sank. "I'm sorry to hear that Martin. These memories from your family... are they what's keeping you awake?"

Martin nodded. "Sometimes I have a dream... Where I'm trapped in this fenced-in yard, and he's walking alongside the perimeter. It's... it's one of the camps. You know? And then... I call out to him, and he can't hear me."

"He's just crying out my name as he walks along, and I'm right next to him begging his attention, and he just keeps shouting for his brother. And then, there's this train track which stays underneath his feet as he walks, and after just enough panic sets in, the train starts coming."

"And he doesn't see it either. We both stop walking, and I see there's this lever that will divert the train and I just can't reach it from that side of the fence and I'm screaming at him to pull it but he's just clueless and it runs him right into the fence and through the camp and I'm free... but feel more trapped than ever as I go to hold his body. Trapped in a future where I'll never see him again. And then I wake up, and I remember how the worst of it is true."

Leveigh leaned forward. "I'm sorry this is happening to you; I want to ask—you used to deny the historical facticity of the Holocaust, isn't that right Martin? I'm sorry you're going through this, but both the loss of your brother and the genocide of my people are in the foreground of your mind, and I don't want to lose track of that connection."

The Corporal sat back at ease, but Martin began to tear up. "I didn't know the whole history, when I drew that symbol on the synagogue, you know? It happened so long ago I just didn't..." He began. "I've apologized to the community, and they were so kind to me. Invited me to pray with them, but I couldn't. The shame wore on me like a cloud whenever I even got near the space. Rabbi Heschel is meeting with me tomorrow to discuss what I can do to relieve this guilt, but I just don't feel like it will ever be enough," his eyes briefly caught Leveigh's before they were diverted once more. "I'm so sorry."

The Corporal scratched his head. "Look, I've read your file. I know about the torture you endured through childhood, the assault when you were seven, and the other reported traumas throughout your life. Those never got resolved."

"You were in pain. You lashed out, and you hurt a community that seemed to be a convenient target for bearing your anger without repercussion. We can talk about anger, and privilege, and how those two came together to cause you to do this to your neighbors, some of whom are now friends; but that seems rather wearisome to me."

"Keep doing what you're doing. Grieve. Learn. Do better. Help to mend what you have injured, and leave be where you cannot. In the meantime, let's work on healing some of those wounds of yours so that there is more of you to give to others. Scars do not hurt like wounds. Does that sound good to you?" the Corporal asked.

Martin nodded.

"Good."

§XVII

Dawud stood up as Oni walked into the Cafe. "Oni…"

Captain Anagonye smiled faintly. "Dawud, good to see you! Thank you for coming."

The two embraced. "Of course, of course. Where else could I possibly be? I'm just so glad you're okay." her former instructor said.

As they sat down and ordered drinks, rain tapped against the windowpane, blurring the light of the traffic outside.

They ordered drinks as the gentle wash of rainwater planed against the roadways outside as passerby made their way through the city.

Dawud readjusted himself in his seat before speaking in a hushed voice. "What's going on Oni? There's this new security force called the 'Florentine Commission' patrolling the streets and detaining people…"

"They've just announced that you're being tried for… espionage? Treason? They're saying you conspired with rogue agents inside the bureaucracy to blow up the Aeschylus? That you are responsible for the attack on Metropolis? Ridiculous claims. Terrifying claims. Falsehoods, I'm sure, but what does it mean?"

Oni nodded with a sad expression. "It means the Ethocracy has been compromised, and that the next few years will likely be mired with war. Heathrow… well, I guess he was right about that." she looked up to meet Dawud's gaze. "I know you made a connection with him Dawud, but I need you to promise me you'll stay away from him. Heathrow Wilson is dangerous."

Dawud sat back in his chair. "I don't understand. He seemed kind to me, and was such an advocate for you in the public eye. Oni, are you sure?"

Oni ran fingers through her hair with a frustrated sigh. "Yes. Actually, right now it's just about the only thing of which I am sure. I need you to trust me on this old friend. Your life may depend on how these next few weeks unfold. Now is not the time to take risks. And strangely, I'm in less of a position to do anything about it now than ever."

Dawud pursed his lips. "No I understand that you're in no position to —"

"It's more complicated than what you know." Oni interjected.

"Then explain it to me."

"I can't."

Mr. Makgoba's brow furled. "Oni, it sounds like you need allies. What can I do to help?"

She blinked. "Stay alive. Bide your time. And then, when no attention is on you, find your way to the gathering at Three Waters."

Dawud fumbled a pen between his fingers. "Three waters? As in Scotland? Why there?"

"That is where the Vanguard has regrouped. You will be safe there. If you leave now, it'll look suspicious. Give it a few days, then make your way to the United Kingdom as discreetly as you can."

Mr. Makgoba leaned forward in his chair. "Oni, you have to explain more. You're frightening me, I-I need to know—"

Oni put her hand on his shoulder. "Do you trust me?" Dawud nodded, and then she continued with a honey-tinged reassurance. "Then believe that I will take care of you, but you have to help me. And to do that, you need to do what I say." she said, a tear slipping from her cheek.

"Okay? Can you do that for me? I promise I'll have more answers for you when next we see each other."

Just then, Thea and Leveigh came through the door. The former spoke up as they reached Oni's table. "It's time. Sorry Dawud."

§XVIC

"So, when are we going to talk about what happened?"

"When we're safe at Three Waters."

"So the public doesn't get to know what she's capable of?"

"Not yet."

"I think that's the wrong decision."

"All that matters is that it's my decision. Understood Corporal?"

"Yes ma'am."

The stage-light glistened as Oni, Thea, and Leveigh stepped into view of the cameras. They took a couch opposite the chair of a short-haired woman in a smart blue dress.

"Hello, and welcome to WT2N, the World Televised News Network." the woman spoke to the audience. "I am your host Cheyenne Biggs, and today we have the solemn task of speaking to K10 Theta, the Vanguards who are now under investigation for the deaths of several thousand colleagues as well as the destruction of the Aeschylus."

"If found guilty, they will almost certainly spend the rest of their lives in exile and house arrest, or worse if the new emergency government changes regulations for criminal sentencing."

"I remind the viewers, who may feel deeply emotional, that our aim here is to understand K10's perspective and reasoning. In keeping with the conduct code for media discourse, our job is to give a platform for the public's intake and comprehension of crucial information."

"While an independent and impartial investigation into these affairs is being conducted, we invite our audience to view briefs from the defendants and prosecution on their intentions, motivations, and actions. Tomorrow, the court proceedings will commence, which will also be televised by WTN."

"With these priorities in-hand, I'd like to welcome K10 Theta and ask them the question on everyone's mind—did you do it? If so, why, and if not—then why is the government accusing you?"

They sat for a moment in uncomfortable silence before Flight Officer Beckett spoke up. "We were not responsible for the destruction of the Aeschylus or any of our beloved colleagues. We did not conspire against the health and success of the Ethocracy; we were investigating a possible lead on the corruption of key officials in the government which was then framed to look like espionage under the guise of the old doctrine of Sovereignty—"

Cheyenne interjected. "I'm sorry, for those who don't know what that is; could you explain what you mean by 'the old doctrine of Sovereignty'?"

Thea looked to Oni, who replied. "Put simply, it's von Galen's term for the way that the state used to legitimize violence against the people by claiming that although the government was 'for the people', sovereignty was vested in leadership, and not the masses. The Ethocracy rejects this claim on principle, and vests individual citizens with absolute authority and access to inquire into the doings of their government without hindrance."

"We will be seeking to prove in court that our intentions were for the health of the Republic, not its undoing as the Senatorial leadership is claiming, and that the charge of espionage is a farce crafted to put us in suspicion of attacking our own people, whom we love deeply. Today we grieve along with the rest of humanity at the loss of our friends and colleagues who were murdered in the attack on the Aeschylus."

Cheyenne passed a box of tissues to the members of K10. "Okay. As you can probably imagine, this is a lot for the public to digest: the single largest attack on our government since the von Galen affair, and you, the accused, suggesting that there is a conspiracy."

"And we are wont to believe you, because you are Vanguards. So far, no Vanguard has come out against you. Indeed, every other Vanguard in the world is still missing in action, many of whom are presumed dead. Do you have any information to share on that front?"

The lights went out, and the recording feeds all went to blue. The audience gasped.

Leveigh was the first to speak. "Listen up everyone. It's going to be okay. Some people will probably be here in a moment to take us away. Before that happens, we need you to listen very carefully."

"Your government has not and will not forget you. The Vanguard is still alive and has regrouped outside of Metropolis. An insurgency has managed to claim significant apparatus of the State and will pretend to exist in complete legitimacy, mourning the destruction of the Chamber of Discourse aboard the Aeschylus, but it will be doing so with crocodile tears."

Thea jumped in, "Just remember—You are safe—the key to their ploy is to keep the people convinced that theirs is the government of liberation, and that we are the insurgents, and this illusion cannot persist if they make people disappear or do excessive harm to the citizenry. At least not at first. It will all happen by increments."

"Keep each other safe, and your heads down. We will come for you, and once we have secured your safety we will rebuild the structure of government to prevent this from ever happening again. We are so sorry. And we love you."

The doors of every exit clattered open, and a battery of armed and armored field police littered the venue, each with the symbol of a feathery black fleur-de-lis branded on the breast of the tac suit.

Canisters of gas floated out towards the base of the stage and bright flashlights beamed in the faces of K10 Theta.

One at the head of the group spoke up. "K10 Theta, you have breached the public trust. Remand yourself into custody now for pretrial detention or we will activate your ankle bracelets and bring you forcibly."

Oni stood up. "Let's go," she said quietly, and the three of them moved themselves into the custody of the Florentine Commission.

"Don't you find it odd that even as society's material quality of life improves, satisfaction with that life grows ever more wearied? We've become so obsessed with the arguments about which 'materials' to use in building our civilization that we've still forgotten to make its blueprints!"

"The question of 'How do we get there?' anticipates an answer to the former, and far more important one 'what kind of world do we want?' If no such answer exists, then goddamn us, we have traded oceans of blood and tears only for oil and concrete; replacing our dear Mother Earth with some Molochite horror in the process. That process is toxic, and our future is too important to let it remain."

— Edgar von Galen in debate with the President of the Academy of the United Nations

Chapter Seventeen

§XVIIA

The courtroom was dim and musty. A cadre of Senators sat in an arc around the long, curved arch of the far wall, which was illuminated mostly by the windows adjacent to the adjudicating panel that overlooked the Vanguards of K10 Theta.

"You have no right to threaten penalty of death," Oni called out to her peers across the floor. "That is not a privilege of the courts, or a permissible function of the state. Von Galen is explicit about the forbiddance of capital punishment."

Silence hung over the proceedings like a drop of poison lingering over them before one member of the tribunal spoke with a seethed roughness.

"You are aware of the provision for life-taking in moments of immediate crisis. Due to the uniquely capricious nature of your activities, allowing you to live presents a grave threat to the livelihoods of many. We all know what you're capable of. If you can prove your innocence, you will be spared."

Another speaker joined in. "The charge is clear: there is abundant evidence to show that K10 Theta collaborated with adversaries of the government to bring about the destruction of the Aeschylus."

"Closed circuit footage shows their infiltration of the Prometheus in an attempt to destroy our station of government, and subsequently the Machiavellian operative, codename Ravenous Thane facilitating their escape. What have you the defendants to say about these allegations?"

Leveigh cleared his throat. "How can we answer an allegation when the intent is the punishment, and not the light of truth? Your viciousness says it for us—we are not guilty."

"Spare us your editorialisms, Corporal Simoneau." said the court. "They will not save you. You may now make your case, for whatever closure it might give you."

Thea spoke plainly. "And what of our right to a public trial? I don't see any cameras, nor would it be appropriate by any Ethocratic statutes to hold our hearing in an abandoned property of a government from the Era of Subjugation. We already know who is really holding us, so let's dispense with the formalities shall we?"

The biting words lingered in the air. "Very well," the court replied. "Since you have decided not to contest the charges, you will be brought before this committee and executed with the utmost prejudice."

Several of the Florentine Commission escorted K10 Theta to the front of the room.

"Hey, we're running out of time here." Leveigh whispered to Oni. "you gonna pull the trigger before they do?"

Thea leaned in. "She'll do what we need when we need it. Trust her."

They were lowered to kneel before the tribunal. Oni could feel the Light Eternal pulse within her. She squeezed her hand, stemming the tide of energy coursing through her body.

"Kill them," ordered the Court.

The windows on the high wall shattered, and a chorus of Vanguards vaulted into the oaken chamber. Oni floated into the air, expelling a forceful burst which cast their executioners into the empty pews behind them.

Scrambling to regain their footing, the remaining soldiers opened fire. As they shot at K10, a battery of Vanguard surrounded their objective, shielding them from the barrage of lead with their energy shielding. The Court quickly fled behind the stands, disappearing into the quarters therein.

§XVIIB

"Heathrow," Shadow called from out the void of the ruined Aeschylus.

The Ravenous Thane drifted through space, floating by marginal increments towards a transport vessel. The visor of his suit blared with alarms—'*low oxygen levels, seek life support refuge at once,*' flashed in red hologram along his periphery.

"Awaken, Thane." The Dark Everlasting called to him. The blackness pooled around him. Ripping apart the casing of his suit in the snap of a second, it crawled into his person as if he were the cosmic vacuum itself. Heathrow's body twitched before falling still.

Several seconds later, his whole body flexed as if renewed with a new, inviolable energy: the armor collapsed back onto his body, and with each reverberation of this vorpal darkness, the size and musculature of his person grew.

"We have much to accomplish."

The citizens of Metropolis spilled out into its urban corridors in a fit of chaos as the Florentine Commission swarmed the surroundings of the corporate district.

"Commander Anagonye, it's good to see you!" one of the line Vanguards yelled over the bustle surrounding them. "We're moving you to a secure location where the Machiavellians were keeping your flightsuits. We've cleared the premises and once you're fitted, we'll be evacuating to the new HQ. My name is Lieutenant Shakespeare. It is an honor to meet you ma'am."

Leveigh and Oni locked gazes as the former mouthed the word, "Commander?" Oni remained wide-eyed, shrugging a shoulder as she returned her attention to their path carved out from the bullets flying by.

"Thanks for the save Lieutenant, but I think you misspoke." Oni replied. "I'm a Captain."

Shakespeare laughed. "Not anymore ma'am," she explained. "A lot has changed. Let's get you back to command and we'll fill you in on everything okay ma'am?"

They rounded the corner into a crammed alleyway.

"Sure," Oni replied, "just stop calling me ma'am please? You're making me feel old."

The Lieutenant shook her head. "I'm pretty sure you're younger than me ma'am, but it's not about age, it's a matter of deference. The suits are right this way... Commander?"

Thea looked at Oni with a grin.

"It's a start." Oni replied, her eyes narrowing at her bemused lover.

Lieutenant Shakespeare gestured at a run-down door which was shear with the faded brick wall beside them. The Vanguard stood watch as they entered. Shakespeare snagged Corporal Simoneau's shirt as he went to walk in after Thea and Oni.

"It's a one room space and they're going to have to strip down. Give them some privacy Corporal."

Leveigh nodded. "So... I'm still a Corporal then?"

Shakespeare looked around before nodding.

"Right," he sighed. "Shakespeare..." the Corporal drummed on, "that's an interesting surname. Write any sonnets lately?"

The Lieutenant scratched her head. "Actually it's my given name. My mum had... high hopes for me. The last name's... von Goethe."

Leveigh grinned.

"Shut up."

The Corporal motioned his hand non-threateningly. "My apologies, no. It caught me by surprise. But I hope your mother is quite proud. Being a Vanguard is really valuable to society and culture. You have done many wonderful things to end up here."

The Lieutenant smiled. "Thanks. I appreciate that. I'm sure she would be."

Oni and Thea emerged from the room, and after Leveigh went in and changed into his gear, they huddled with the remaining Vanguard. Oni gestured to von Goethe. "Fill me in Lieutenant. What's the situation based on current Vanguard intelligence?"

Shakespeare nodded. "Yes Commander. First, the unknown quantities —although it is clear that there has been a Machiavellian takeover of the Senate, we do not know how deeply embedded these operatives are, nor who they are. Based on your research, we know that senators Watkins, Strauss, and McKinley are culpable, but so far we have no other leads."

Oni interjected. "Senator Wilson. Heathrow Wilson… is the Ravenous Thane. I saw his face wearing the raven-clad armor with my own eyes. If he's still alive, he is definitely a part of Machiavellian leadership. We've had eyes on him, Ravenous Claw and Bow during this operation. Still no word about a 'Ravenous Legion'?"

This time, another Vanguard spoke, "no ma'am, so far it's just a name on the wind. Our intelligence still has yet to independently confirm the existence of a fourth member. Corporal Leveigh, we will need access to the Archive data to determine what more can be gleaned about the person in question."

Leveigh cleared his throat, slowly standing into the center of discourse. "That's… going to be tricky," he explained softly, gazing at Oni, then back to the Vanguard who had addressed him. "We know of someone who has access to—"

"It's not a problem." Corvin answered, appearing before them in a wisp of smoke. He held Dawud in his arms—eyes closed and covered with a film of dust—deep, purple bruises across his head, neck, and hands, with a tattered shirt to match. "He'll be okay," said Corvin. Handing Oni's former instructor into her capable arms, he continued.

"Listen, you all undoubtedly have many questions about who I am, what you've just witnessed, and how I can give you this," he began, conjuring a briefcase out of thin air before handing it to Shakespeare. Corvin looked at the Lieutenant solemnly. "You will find all the information and authentication you need in there to confidently indict almost every living Senator."

Leveigh shook his head. "That can't be right. Many of our colleagues aboard the Prometheus are—"

"Dead, Mr. Simoneau." said Corvin, "many of your colleagues were purged as soon as you left the premises."

"That's horrible." Leveigh replied. Without turning his head, the Corporal leaned in towards Thea. "it's doctor though, actually." he whispered.

Thea's face stayed level as she side-eyed her friend. "I don't think gods tend to fuss about credentialing very much."

"Right." Leveigh nodded stiffly. "Makes sense."

Corvin walked to the edge of the oblong gathering, turning about face to address everyone there present. "Here's the problem: if you don't trust me, many of you will die right here, right now. I know your plan to evacuate Oni. There are two things which will make your operation terminally inoperable."

"First, that the Machiavellians have since manufactured at least a dozen Quantic blades wielded by elite soldiers wearing rebranded Vanguard tech; most of which are patrolling directly between you and your transports at this time."

The All-Father turned to face Oni. "Now, these will likely not be a threat to you, but I'm afraid something more sinister has awoken, and it is coming. We have to remove you from this scene, and quick. Do you trust me?"

Oni nodded, after which the Vanguard all placed their closed hands over their hearts.

Corvin whisked them out of the world with a wave of his fingers. Stepping out of the alleyway, two figures wearing flightsuits with a florentine emblem called out to him, Quantic blades in-hand. Corvin smiled as they approached, white-gold light shining out from his eyes like the polished basin of a saintly grail.

"Resistance is the protest of those who hope, and hope is the feast of the people who resist."

— Jurgen Moltmann, *The Power of the Powerless*

Chapter Eighteen

§XVIIIA

The caravan stretched along a swath of eroded granite, which was nestled in trees and sparse shrubbery under the purview of the umber mountains. Great blankets of white tumbled over a blue-grey sky, which spilled the scent of damp greenery and clay into and through the valley.

The peppering calls of black grouse hung over the grassland, much like the morning chill which held it as with bony fingers; clinging under the flightsuits of K10 Theta and the Vanguard as if their armor were of thin and flimsy cloth. Yet the aura was bracing; urgent even, and the wild's call was a fitting veil for this auspicious day.

The cameras were rolling, as all the Vanguard watched on with bated breath.

"People of the world," Oni began, perched on a stool.

"It is with great sadness that I inform you that your government has been compromised. The original intent of the Ethocracy was to elevate the status of civilization to one of harmony and depth of meaning; full stomachs, bright futures, continual education, universal healthcare, sustainable energy, and meaningful work balanced with plenty of time for family and friends."

"These were our ideals. But, like Icarus, we flew as high as our wings could take us without considering the dangers. Our hubris cost us dearly, and now I am duty-bound to tell you—agents in favor of the old doctrine of nation-state have taken over the halls of power, retain control of our Capitol in Metropolis, destroyed the Halls of Discourse aboard the Aeschylus murdering thousands of Vanguards, and have co-opted the Senate for their own use."

"Soon, they will cease pretending that these are temporary, emergency powers. You will be under authoritarian rule, whatever they may call it. But we ask you to be brave; there are 300 of us Vanguard remaining, and that is more than enough to topple these pretenders."

"It is unclear what their policy goals are, and we do not know who will be relatively safe, and who they will target as 'the other.' And they will do that; it is in the nature of Fascists to stir up the fears of decent folk in service of a malignant cause. It will be on each of you to resist the fear-mongering, and to continue listening to the fruits of love our work together has fostered among all peoples in the Ethocratic state."

"These cruel oligarchs would have us return to a sharp division of prosperity and freedom between the powerful, namely themselves, and everyone else. They do not share society's modern compassionate vision, and seek to break our autonomy and intention into submission and obedience. They wish to forge our destinies for us, but I promise you this—you shall not dwell long in the shadow of Prometheus."

"The Vanguard will rebuild and flourish, and once we have taken back the halls of power, we will rebuild the Ethocracy in such a way that nothing like this can ever happen again. We have failed you, and for this our hearts ache—but we will vindicate your belief in us. We will come for you. Stay strong. You are loved." she finished, placing her closed hand across her heart.

Once the recording was finished and the cameras were taken away, her audience came into full-circle around her.

"Well, what'd you all think?" Oni asked. "Was that fine? I'm never any good at those sorts of things."

A voice called out somewhere in the back row. "It'll be great Commander."

Another beckoned, "Now we just have to figure out how to convince ourselves this will work." There was some laughter, though not all was out of humor. Tension still hung thick over the air.

Shakespeare stepped forward. "Commander, I think we all need to know… How did you get off the Aeschylus? It seemed to have been an impossible task. We were all stunned to hear K10 Theta was under arrest in Metropolis… From the events that unfolded during our operation earlier today, I think it's clear that there's more going on here than we currently know."

Oni nodded. "Yes. It's not the sort of thing I can just tell you… It's probably best if I show you. What you're about to see might be very frightening. But you've all trusted me this far." she said, floating into the air without the use of her flight-suit tech. The suit's plating drifted off her body like magnets repelling in the air. "So I only ask that you trust me this one step farther. All will be clear."

Her dæmon form emerged, the blue energy pulsing in her eyes and veins, tinting the cloth of her undersuit a deep cobalt. Oni pointed to the Sun, which seemed to vanish.

"Vanguards, see as I see." she called out. The dim horn of the Light

Eternal reverberated throughout the landscape. The stars in the sky swirled like dust in the wind. Oni snapped her fingers, and a bold whiteness filled the air, making the shine of the stars brush an amber stain across the light. The forms morphed along with the words Oni spoke, articulating images across the wide breadth of mother Earth.

"There was always the Light, and forever has she longed for what we shall become. Crafting herself in the form of our foundation through eons inside the womb of her boundless galaxies, she birthed us in such a state as to cull the limits of natural law and give rise to the temple of our own wanting."

"But the moment of that umbilical breakage of our selfhood from out of her form became a symbol in our minds, and rather than absorbing fully the character and significance of our selfhood, we saw only the violence through which we were begotten— a darkness everlasting, the scar of our tender entrance into the world and the foothold of 'existence' as we know it."

"Yet the deeper grain of the Light's intent remains within us; sometimes the seed germinates, and sometimes, its flower spreads. One such seedling has been vested in me through a branch of the Light Eternal, the one some of you have met called Corvin."

Oni looked down to see Thea leaving the circle, walking down towards the encampment. Gradually, she floated down to the earth as she concluded. "You all have a lot to process. Examine the contents of the dossier, access my suit's recording memory and those of your peers who came to liberate us. You will find the information you need." And with that, Oni returned to her normal countenance.

"Be back here at 18:00 for our briefing for the fight to come. Dismissed." she said, following after the trail of her lover.

When Oni entered the private quarters, she saw Thea with her head clasped in her hands. "Hey, what's going on? You can talk to me Thea."

Flight Officer Beckett turned to face Oni. "Can I?"

Oni grimaced. "It's me, love. I'm here for you."

Thea shook her head. "I know it's going to feel different for you, but can you try to understand why I might a little distressed by how all this has unfolded? I don't even know how much of you… is really you anymore."

Oni kneeled to be even with Thea. "I'm sorry you feel that way," she said. "I can only speak from my own experience, but I can tell you… while a lot has happened to me, it's still me, love. I'm still your girl."

Thea winced. "I'm sorry. So sorry. It's just, with everything that has happened… I haven't even grieved the death of Michael yet, you know? When I even stop to think about what we've been through, I just feel sick, like there's this knot in my stomach and, when I look at you… it lessens, and I'm at peace."

"You're my anchor, and the waves are tossing, and I'm just praying that you hold me down so that I don't get lost in this storm. So if it is you, I need you to close your eyes," she pleaded.

They were both trembling slightly as Oni did what she asked. "Next," Thea continued, sitting up from beside her. "I need you to breathe in, hold, and as you breathe out, meet my eyes with yours."

Oni's face flashed brightly, a tear pooling softly across her face as Thea held a plain silver ring in front of her, standing on both knees.

Beckett laughed nervously, and then opened her mouth to flower her love with a smile. "Oni Anagonye, my love… will you marry me?"

The Commander's smile faded slightly. "Thea, every fiber of my heart wants to say yes. But I need to know… are you asking because you're afraid of losing me, or because this is something you've been carrying in your heart?"

Thea smiled, turning her head to the side. Oni's face softened.

"Yes," she answered, "with all that I am, I will marry you Thea Mae Beckett."

§ XVIIIC

Corvin pounded through the air of the caravan, walking at a breakneck pace. "ONI." he yelled. "Where is she?" he demanded, looking around wildly.

Leveigh, who was perusing the contents of the dossier, stood up to greet him. "Corvin!" he called out brightly. "What's the matter? She's busy but I'll alert her to your presence now."

He turned his head. "Hey, Aeschylus?"

"*Yes Leveigh?*" the AI's voice chimed in.

"Send for Oni. Priority one." the Corporal replied.

"*The Commander has been contacted.*" said Aeschylus.

"Thank you." answered the Corporal, turning once again to face Corvin. "Alright, she's on her way soon. What's going on Corvin?"

The All-Father looked off in the distance. "They actually did it." he whispered.

"Sorry," said Leveigh, "could you be somewhat more specific?"

Corvin turned to meet his gaze. "They bombed Metropolis. Thousands dead."

Leveigh's eyes widened. "What? Why? They already had control of the city."

Corvin took a seat. "Now they also have control of the people. Who do you think they're going to blame for this? Few residents of Metropolis will trust the Vanguard now."

"Nor should they." Oni finished, walking up to meet Corvin. "Even if they can deduce that we didn't bomb them, we still allowed for all this to happen, and until we retain order we are no longer a quorum. Our actions are not democratic."

"We are no more a government than an insurgency now," she stood next to the All-Father, "And we must simply hope that we retain decent favor in the rest of our territories, fervently working to earn their trust again."

She turned her head to address the Vanguard. "Alright everyone, we've got no time to lose. Gear up, and we'll leave for Metropolis tonight. The Machiavellians, the Ravenous… We end them before the sun rises, understood? Corvin, I—"

The All-Father placed his hand on Oni's shoulder, and the two of them stood on the moon once more.

"Corvin, Jesus! You can't just keep taking us here!" she yelled.

"Oni I—" Ratzinger began.

"Bring us back. I'd do it myself but I'm still figuring out how this stuff works," said Oni curtly.

"We have a problem." the All-Father began, lifting his coat to reveal a gouging wound at his waist.

"What?" Oni stammered, her eyes widening as she watched the immortal collapse.

"It is from out of a fundamental misapprehension that the academician tries to make a science of human nature. What humankind has been doing is a fundamentally different question from 'of what are they capable?' Surely, the illusion is comforting: to believe that by putting human volition under a microscope and dissecting its organonical constitution with the penetrating discipline of skeptical inquiry—that somehow, the defects could all be identified and excised."

"Alas the truth is not so simple, as the scores of millions of graves from the conflicts of the 21st century well attest. Their faith in fatalism coaxed them into a wretched complacency and consigned them to decades of needless misery."

"Learning from their failures, the onus is on each of us to reject both polls and opinion as meritorious sources of political wisdom; operating under the awareness that neither science nor idle speculation can help us here."

"Rather, the only institutional endeavor worth preserving is the polico-ethical permeation of that perennial ponderance 'what ought I do?' And under the guidance of that striving, under the consent of the commons to enter into the contract of civilization; to foment the unravelling of the bonds of our subjugation from each arm, and to march unhesitatingly towards our destined birthright— that is, unequivocally, Utopia."

— Edgar von Galen, *The Ethocracy*

§XIXA

With a quick brush of her hand, Oni closed the wound. Corvin coughed gently as he sat up, pacing himself with shallow breaths.

"How did this happen?" said Oni.

Corvin groaned. "These Florentine Commission guys know their stuff… I was trying to thin out the herd of Quantic tech wielders before the operation. Too many casualties already. I managed to take down most of them, but then I got stuck by one," he said, grasping his hip. "And, well… it stuck."

Oni's brow sunk. "Did something change? I mean that's odd, right?"

"Very," Corvin said, but his tone seemed steady; resigned, even. "If it weren't for the fact that I relinquished half of my power recently."

Oni's eyes raised in shock. "Wait, this is happening because of me? Because you gave me access to the Light?"

The All-Father shook his head. "No, no Oni. You mustn't blame yourself. It is not to do with what I have passed onto you; the Light can embrace whomsoever it chooses. But, there's… something you must know."

He turned to face the sun. "Fuck this is going to be hard." Corvin whispered.

Oni walked behind him, placing her hand on his shoulder. "Look: however strange and off-putting this relationship has been… I've come to see a side of you that is good. Whatever you're about to tell me—I promise you I will hear it, and that after it has been heard, I will still respect you and value your well-being. Understood?"

Corvin nodded slowly. "Well, it's not as if I had a choice. The fate of everything… Either I could be the enemy, or I could…" he trailed off, stifling a tear. "Or I could face the Darkness of my causing, and be authentic towards my calling as a child of the Light."

He turned to face her. "I chose the latter. And it means that now I am, like you, merely dæmon."

Oni shook head with a penetrating stare, "I don't understand."

"Well," Corvin replied, "the deeper nature of the force to which I was tied, that of the All-Father, was tainted with… something. A being by the name of El who was the forbearer of this title, had held in him the whole duality of the Universe in a primordial state: that of the Light Eternal, and also of the Dark."

"Bearing his darkness as an essential quality, El was just as happy to bring more pain into the world if it furthered his own vision. Now, this is not an essentially sinister quality—indeed, life on Earth germinated from such workings. The whole of your science's 'Evolution' is predicated on the wheel of progress through pain."

"And yet, ultimately El was only ever interested in supremacy over these creatures. Bound up with both the light and the dark, he was able to dictate the course of history towards his own ends for millennia, even as it grew away from the promise of the Light through which this Universe was born."

Oni hesitated. "So, you've broken this hegemony of the All-Father?" Corvin nodded. "Okay," she continued. "What does that mean for us though?"

Corvin frowned. "It means that the Darkness is out there now. It seems that rather than accepting my volition in the matter, El has allowed All-Father to have something of a psychotic schism. He is out there, right now, likely looking for the nearest willing host; and the both of us are only endowed with half the power of this cosmic force."

Anagonye's heart sank. "Where were you when this happened?"

Corvin pointed downwards as Oni's mouth went dry. "It's almost certain that Heathrow Wilson was the nearest living subject. Are you telling me that the Ravenous Thane is like us now?"

Corvin nodded. "Yes, that is exactly what I'm telling you. That's why I came out here in the first place, actually."

Oni pulled her hair along the side of her head. "Corvin, no! Wilson is the last person in the world we want having that kind of power. Don't you understand?"

"Oni," Corvin replied. "It is because I understand that I have done this. No matter who the Darkness infects, it will be an ominous and foreboding opponent. Heathrow is a dangerous man, and a powerful political adversary… But so long as we contain our worries to stopping him, we have an advantage. If it comes to a direct confrontation, there are two of us, and only one of him."

Oni sighed in frustration. "Okay, then give me the rest of the Light. I will take care of this. The stakes are too high to hesitate any longer, right?"

Corvin shook his head. "Sorry, it doesn't work like that. You accepted as much of the Light as you were able to at the time of your initiation. And besides, as you see, I am rather tapped-out now. For better or worse, you will have to grow into your powers before claiming divinity."

Oni's arms sunk. "You know… it probably would have been helpful to keep me in the loop on this."

The All-Father seemed taken aback. "Forgive me. I come from another time. There weren't really women like you from where I come. I'm not used to consulting them."

"There were," Oni replied curtly. "Society just does less to quiet them now."

Ratzinger averted his eyes. "Sorry. You're right, of course. Will you pardon this old fool?" he said with a faint smile.

"Interpret this eye-roll however you'd like," said Oni, gesturing for emphasis, "we've got too much on our hands to get into it now. So what's our plan?"

Corvin walked half-circle around the Vanguard in contemplation. "For a start, I need time. Time to commune with the Light now unfiltered within me. I have been spiritually gutted, and must regain myself before I confront what comes before us. You do what needs to be done. I will be there and ready when the time comes." he said, opening a portal to snow-strewn mountains.

"And if I am to face the Ravenous Thane before you are ready?" Oni asked.

"You won't," Corvin answered, and with that the All-Father ducked into the mountainside and out of sight, the portal closing behind him.

Oni looked upon the pale blue dot. With decreasing hesitance, she became dæmon: floating gradually earthwards before warping back to Three Waters in a streak of azure light.

§XIXB

As she materialized before the Vanguard, there was some disorder among the rank and file. Thea and Corporal Simoneau were quick to come to her side.

"Where did you and Corvin go? We were worried about you," Leveigh opened.

"No time," said Oni.

Thea's eyes widened. "No; Oni we need to know what's going on."

The Commander vaulted into the air, projecting her voice with a supernatural bang of energy, igniting the landscape with motion as she spoke. "Vanguards—there has been an unprecedented assault on our Ethocracy and its people, who are all the human race. We go now, we fight the Machiavellians in whatever form they take, and we take back the Capitol. Understood?"

All the Vanguard raised their fists over their hearts, though Thea and Leveigh moved to form somewhat more slowly.

"Good. Now move out."

§XIXC

The voice of El called out, feathered by the pounding wind of the mountainside, "Corvin. Well come, old friend."

While the old one spoke, Corvin scaled the familiar path towards the mountain's caldera. "We are not friends, shadow. You know why I have come here. Let's not play games."

A lull in the wind emerged, bringing with perfect clarity the rumbling landscape's creaks and roars to the foreground. "Very well." the voice emanated.

A colossal spread of vines sprang out of the ground before him, churning into a form familiar to its adversary—the likeness of a leopard. Tall as a statue, the mimetic figure also bore the representation of every wound Corvin had dealt its origin on his path to ascendance, as well as the presumable decay of its corpse.

Blood seeped out of the crevices of the latticing between the weave of each vine, staining the wood a dark, rusty hue; and deep in its eyes, among dimly singed coils, were tempestuous spires of flame. The titanous creature howled, stirring flakes of snow through the air in a whirlpool of violent signification.

"Your sins come back to haunt you, Elrick." the voice of El beckoned.

Corvin reached out his hand, the hammer of the tree glimmering into shape with a sweeping arc of light. And then he leapt.

The blow shattered a large swath of the golem's shoulder and neck, but as the coils of root continued to shoot out of the ground, it quickly regained its full form. The elemental grabbed Corvin before he could regain his footing and slammed him into the mountainside.

Stone dust and rubble ricocheted around them, blurring view of the range beyond. The All-Father slipped loose of the creature's hold, coughing up blood as he stumbled away. The totem lurched, then jolted towards the dæmon once more.

In a series of swift teleportations, over and over again, Corvin fell into the beast, slamming the hammer into its body with all of his might. Yet as fast as he could muster these blows, the body of the being regenerated.

El laughed. "Nothing I've taught you will save you from this creature. You will not come face to face with me again. This is no proving ground. Turn away, return to the war front, and face my progeny."

Corvin apparated some distance from the monstrosity. Closing his eyes and vanishing his hammer, the All-Father stood motionless except for a gentle swaying with the wind. He brought his hands clasped together. As the thing bounded towards him, he remained steadfast.

"Consigning your fate to the dustbin of history? Oh Corvin, I am almost disappointed." the voice of El sneered, "I had hoped for your death to be a christening for my legacy in the person of Heathrow Wilson. No matter."

Corvin opened his eyes, meeting the gaze of the totem before him. "I'm sorry," he whispered. "Let me finally lay you down to rest, sweet creature."

Great tendrils of radiant white-gold energy sprung out from behind Corvin like the ligaments of wings. As the golem careened from above, Corvin extended his arms and body forward as the tendrils shot into each crevice of the roots' ornate weave, branching out through its figure and filling the hollow portions of its body with light.

Pulling his arms out full-span, the beast was torn apart as the energy ripped back out to Corvin's sides. The All-Father sprinted forwards towards the alcove and the pathway to the icy caldera.

As he bulleted towards the tree at a breakneck pace, its roots dislodged, once again transforming into molten iron. Yet this time, instead of reaching out to grab Corvin, they lunged at him, one after another like spears seeking out a chink in the armor of their opponent. The beams of energy wrapped around Corvin tightly, mimicking the trajectories of each root at it came for him.

The floor of the caldera began to give way to thick veins of magma, and just as the All-Father saw his footing begin to slip, he rocketed in the air towards trunk of the tree. Corvin Elrick called out the hammer once more to his grasp. The roots recoiled from their assault as he did so, bundling all around the tree in a tight network of barbs and spikes.

Corvin blinked, portaling onto the other side of that emergent mesh of iron. Quickly, he hustled the hammer back onto the bark of its trunk, and suddenly all was at rest. The roots relaxed and regained their previous form, and the floor of the caldera settled as the weapon was absorbed once more into the wood.

Corvin's breath and the wind were as one, and with a cosmic eye he could see the whole of the mountain-scape settle like a veil floating down onto the Earth. The rim of the caldera faltered as the sky cleared to blue lightness. Birds sang, the air was sweet and the light tender as it graced his skin. A flowered meadow replaced the desolate landscape as the rim of the caldera yielded, making the tree to be as if a signpost on the top of a gradual hill. The leaves of its branches flourished and transformed, rustling in their play with the now-tamed wind.

"What have you done?" the voice of El called out, uncertain.

The All-Father walked up to the tree trunk, resting his palms in the marbled contours of its wood. "I could rest here forever," Corvin began, "but I have the lives of many depending on me." The tendrils of light poured back into him, and through his hands into the trunk of the tree.

"So," Ratzinger continued, "we're going to have a brief hundred-year chat in a pocket dimension," he said, casting a circle of light around him and the tree. "And then, when that's done, I will clean up whatever's left of you in the world."

Great bodhi leaves shimmered as Corvin nestled himself against a crease in the roots. A warm gust soothed him as a smile floated up onto his person. He buckled his legs tight up against the seat of his pants, and breathed deeply. An aura of peaceful lightness welled up from out of the All-Father as the countryside rustled in anticipation.

"Hence, in seizing a state, the attacker ought to examine closely all those injuries which are necessary, and to do them all at one stroke so as not to have to repeat them daily. Thus by not continually upsetting the people, he will be able to make them feel more secure, and win them over by benefits."

"He who does otherwise… is always forced to keep the knife in his hand. He cannot rely on his subjects, and they cannot attach themselves to him, because of the continued and repeated wrongs. Injuries ought to be done all at one time, so that, being tasted less, they offend less. Benefits ought to be given little by little, so that their flavour may last longer."

—Machiavelli, *The Prince*

Chapter Twenty

§XXA

Metropolis had been torn asunder. The sky was meshed with rolling grey pillars of smoke that shone amber from the light of a hundred fires scattered throughout the streets, and it was in the center of that calamity that the transport ships dropped the Vanguard swiftly by the overpass at Ravenna Boulevard.

"Alright Vanguards, head towards the WT2N station for broadcast." Oni called out. She stepped confidently, only wearing the neutral leotard on which the flight-suit normally perched.

"K10 Theta will join the rest of the surviving K block in providing overwatch spotting, logistics, and support. If we encounter any Ravenous, leave them to me and get yourself to safety. The world needs you alive. Okay, move out!"

They fanned out into the street quickly, and K block took to the roof tops, peering down each offshoot street and alleyway as they passed.

When they arrived at the media outlet, K10 scouted out ahead towards the entrance.

"Looks like we've got company," von Goethe called out over the Porta-COMs.

Sweeping in from either end of the block were a battery of soldiers of the Florentine commission, three of whom carried Quantic tech—two elite ground troops with swords, and the Ravenous Claw, all of whom wore modified flight-suit tech and the fleur-de-lis brand.

Oni turned to the Vanguard. "K block, you go in and make sure the video gets out there. K10, I'm going to need you two to take the helm on this one, okay?" Her compatriots nodded before she continued.

"The rest of the Vanguard, disperse. Clear the fires. Disarm the Machiavellians. Rally the public to safety, and stay safe. I'll take care of these." she said, gesturing to the opposition flanking them.

About a dozen Vanguard followed Thea and Leveigh into the building, the rest launching off in a barrage, into the smoke and out of view.

Oni walked forward to the intersection of the street. "You have just murdered thousands of citizens who put their faith in the Ethocracy to protect them. There is no redemption for you." she bellowed, shaking with rage. She clenched her fists, and with a strike of azure lightning became dæmon, her eyes pulsing with a dire and vehement gaze. The marching wavered.

"You have only one choice now," she continued. "Lay down your weapons, and I will detain you until we find some hole big enough to throw you in. Otherwise…" she said, turning her head at the front guard of the Florentines. "I will cull you all with the same incautionate abandon with which you took our people from the world."

The Florentine commission opened fire. With a brush of her hands, the bullets all caught in a vortex field around her, each spinning in orbit as if still seeking their target. Ignoring them, Oni pinched towards the ashen sky, and a dusty cloud swirled down to saturate the facing of the WT2N tower with a dark and opaque haze.

The shooting settled as the cloud which surrounded the building sparked with bolts of ambient light. Casting her hand over towards a neighboring skyscraper, the bullets ejected from around her, scraping the face of the building and tearing up hundreds of thousands of large plexiglass shards. Then, with another simple gesture, the lead and glass surrounded the Florentine Commission on either side as a ragged and vitally impassible field.

Oni filled the theater of combat with a mulled voice that reverberated as if directly spoken through the wind of their ears. "Step out of the barrier, or fire so much as another bullet, and you will have only harmed yourself. Stay where you are if you value your life."

Claw and the two Florentine stepped forward with their Quantic weaponry, the projectiles fizzling out from the energy fields of their specialized suits as they approached the young Vanguard Commander. As the few of them charged forward, and with zero hesitation— Oni snapped her fingers.

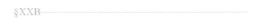

§XXB

The lobby was empty as the K block Vanguard moved towards the stairwell. Lights flickered, and the air was still.

"Be careful, Vanguard." Thea cautioned, "We don't know who has access to Quantic tech or if there is an EMP device on-sight. For all we know, we're sitting ducks. Be ready to evacuate."

As they stormed the stairwell, a desperate calamity could be heard on the levels of the WT2N tower up ahead. Thea looked to Leveigh, who nodded almost instantly.

"Vanguards, fan out. Get civilians down to the basement and protect them. K10 will complete the mission," she instructed. As the Flight Officer spoke, she and Leveigh straddled the railing of the boxed stairwell, and in short order rocketed themselves to the top floor. As they got to the entrance, they confronted a cadre of Florentine soldiers trying to breach the door.

Several bullets flew in the time that it took for Thea and Leveigh to dismantle the opposition—jaws, temples and necks swiftly struck into futility as the remainder of them were grappled into the unforgiving concrete. Leveigh punched his straightened hand through the crevice of the door, ripping it from the hinges which affixed it to the wall.

As the macabre sight came into view, a shadow floated between the building and the outside world. They could hear the gunshots and screams from outside. This time, Leveigh turned to Thea.

"Oni is out there. It will be okay. Our job is here. We can't get distracted now," she said. Leveigh nodded.

The room was a telecasting studio, with server towers, screens and control panels littering the space around them. Front and center, Cheyenne Briggs lay stooped across the main control unit: a large-caliber wound having torn through her neck and shoulder: a corresponding hole punctured through the plate of glass ahead.

The blood pooled along the switches and dials and onto the floor, and a prompt sat on the screen: "executive recording command: Air. Review. Delete." With gravitas, Leveigh walked up to the fallen citizen of Metropolis. "So sorry, Cheyenne." As he selected 'air' on the dial, the screens lit up with a recording of the anchor, in the same pantsuit she wore in death.

"Ethocrats the world around," the recording began, "what I have witnessed in these last 24 hours is the most heinous affront to the dignity of humanity since the assassination of Edgar von Galen. As many of you know, WT2N was forcibly taken off-air yesterday by this new 'Florentine Commission', supposedly the temporary stop-gap department for the safety of the public in the absence of the Vanguard. Now I cannot speak to the innocence or guilt of K10 Theta."

"But I must tell you this—the commission has demanded that we submit to an uncorroborated, singular narrative of profoundly anti-democratic values. That the Vanguard and a large majority of the Senate had been corrupt, and so the experiment of democracy, not just von Galen's vision, had failed. That only through the firm rule of law and unchecked guidance of our surviving leaders could we, as they said, 'galvanize our common destiny, and resoundly forsake the perdition of such grave and contemptible transgressions.'"

"Simply put, they wanted our outlet to shift blame onto the people, and for penance to be purchased with the destruction of our rights and freedoms. Once we refused, they pulled the plug from under WT2N on the permanent. Many of my colleagues were taken, god knows where. I don't know why they spared me. Whatever you might hear from their media front, and no matter who might say otherwise: the government is no longer your friend."

"Now through underground channels, this reporter was able to procure a generator powerful enough to transmit this message to you. I will air the recording, and then… at least then I will have done something important before… Well, before they get me. Stay safe, my fellow citizens. Survive, resist, and stay vigilant."

The screens went blank. Then, K10 Theta went to work.

§XXC

The field of bodies plastered the concrete of Ravenna Boulevard.

"Well," called out the Ravenous. "I will admit, I wouldn't have guessed you had it in you, Oni Anagonye." The talon-crescent Quantic blades fitted to his arms sparked menacingly. "What a wonderful narrative you've handed us; a gift, really. I will have to make your death exceptionally quick—as a thank you from yours truly. Legion will be pleased." The two other Quantic wielders flanked Oni. "Kill her," rasped the Ravenous Claw.

The Vanguard Commander whipped her hand towards the nearest elite guard. The Machiavellian's hilt jerked backwards, carving the blade into his head. As he faltered, Oni Anagonye summoned the weapon part way towards her person, then veered it to confront the other bearer of the fleur-de-lis.

With a dizzying series of lashes, the disembodied armament forced the combatant backwards, barely matching the first three swipes of the blade before being butchered by the fourth. Then, Anagonye summoned the two swords just in time to catch an incoming swipe from the Ravenous Claw.

Exchanging a flurry of blows, Oni tossed one blade skywards. Blocking a final few lunges with the sword and a grin, the latter blade crushed through the back of the Ravenous Claw, cleaving him in two as her partners in K10 Theta exited the WT2N building.

As she noticed their presence, she fell out of dæmon form swiftly as she floated to their side.

"Did you get it done?"

Leveigh held his hand behind his head as he and Thea nodded. The latter spoke back in kind, her voice trembling as she pointed to the bodies out behind them, "and what about you? What did you do?"

Oni blinked. "I did what had to be done, to give you the time you needed to get that recording to air. Now the world knows the truth."

"With all due respect Commander," Leveigh replied hesitatingly, "this is not how we conduct our business. They may have done unspeakable things, but their wrongdoing does not necessitate ours, nor would it ever excuse misconduct. Oni... how could you have done this?"

The Commander shook her head. "You don't understand. This is not the end for them. They will be reborn, and when the last of this insurgency is overcome, their futures will know peace. All of ours will. It is as much for their good as ours."

Thea folded her arms. "But you've just gone and done the very worst of what we shame them for. What's the point of even believing in progress if the means by which to attain it perpetuates what is cruel and clearly wrong in the world?"

"Even if what you say is true... the point of our way of doing things is to remake the world in such a way where actions like this have absolutely no place. By perpetuating this violence, you contribute to the regression of society, which has ripples that echo through all history. What we do in the here and now... it matters, profoundly."

"But is this what Corvin has taught you to believe?" Tears streamed down Thea's face as she gestured to the remnants of her lover's slaughter. "Oni, you're breaking my heart."

"I'm sorry." said Oni meekly. "I didn't see another way. There were so many of them and I just acted on instinct. It's like I didn't even know what was happening and then all of the sudden I—" she stammered as a canister landed at their feet. In a pulse of radiation, the mechanics of their flightsuits fried. A second later, a gunshot pierced Leveigh right through the eye.

The next thing the Commander knew, she stood as full-dæmon a mile away on a rooftop, her arm plunged into the chest of the Ravenous Bow as his heart muscle split into ribbons between her fingers.

Half in fear, half in fury, she watched as the light flickered out of his eyes.

As he crumpled to the floor, Oni looked out towards her friends as Thea ran to hold Leveigh. Through all the distance, she viewed them as if they were in arms-reach.

"What am I?" she whispered, vanishing in a gust of wind.

"O brother stand the pain; escape the poison of your impulses. The sky will bow to your beauty, if you do. Learn to light the candle. Rise with the sun. Turn away from the cave of your sleeping. That way a thorn expands into a rose—a particular glows with the Universal."

— Rumi

Chapter Twenty-one

§XXIA

"Ah, you must be Abraham's son!" a voice called out from behind him. Martin sat at a grave outside the Maisel synagogue, placing a bundle of lilac flowers along the span where the headstone met the weathered soil. As his bangs scattered in a gust of wind, he sat back to view the stone's engraving with a sigh.

"Is this your family?" the voice wondered as it came to his side.

"No," Martin replied flatly, "just someone who I feel like I might have known." He turned to face the visitor. A slender man in sunglass spectacles, leather gloves, and a trench coat stood behind him; a scar ragged across his face and mouth.

"I tend the graves here sometimes," Martin continued. "and I always find myself visiting her before I go, though I've never met her. It's strange, I know." Martin sat up, offering his hand. "Sorry, you asked if I was Abraham's son? I'm afraid I don't know an 'Abraham'. You must be looking for someone else. My name is Martin Kempf."

The man in the trench coat pointed towards the Star of David marked along the top of the tombstone. "Just some playfulness. My doctorate was in ministry, so some religious studies humor always tickles me." he said, taking Martin's hand with a firm grasp. "The name's Doctor Friedrich Anagonye. Pleasure to meet you."

Martin shook his head. "I guess the joke went over my head. Apologies, Friedrich."

"Not a worry." Dr. Anagonye replied. "You are a member of the synagogue though, right?"

Air puffed out Martin's cheeks. "No. Actually, I am doing penance for crimes against the jewish community here. I defaced the property with a hate symbol some months ago. I am reformed and have been forgiven by the congregants here, but I still do service to help upkeep the grounds, and in return they have helped me to study the Torah."

"Well," Friedrich replied without missing a beat, "I'm sure the rabbi would say it takes a man of integrity to admit such a past, and to genuinely make amends. Tell me, Mr. Kempf, do you know who I am?" he asked, tucking his spectacles in the breast pocket of his coat.

Martin peered inquisitively. "... Any chance you're related to the Vanguard of the same name?"

The doctor laughed. "Ah, so you've met Oni! Yes, she's my daughter. She's quite something, isn't she?"

Martin's eyes wandered, "she certainly left an impression… Sorry, I just realized—it's past hours. How did you get in here? Let me walk you out. I'm sure the family of a Vanguard can find their own way, but I could get in trouble if I—"

"Oh Martin," Dr. Anagonye muttered. "I had such high hopes for you. A genius IQ, and an exceptional student despite all the world conspiring against your success. The Organization watched you from an early age. Who do you think it was that slipped *Mein Kampf* into your backpack when you were just a boy?"

"Voracious and inquisitive, we were sure it would be only a matter of time before the ideas percolated to fullness in your mind. But... we were wrong. You used his thought as a pathetic catalyst for your miserable, self-indulgent tantrums and abandoned your potential willingly. It was disgusting, really."

Oni's father whipped a luger out of his coat pocket, planting bullets in Martin's stomach and chest. The young man felt the flutters of blood stain his shirt as he stumbled back, leaning against the tombstone for support.

Martin muttered back to Friedrich, "Please... no..."

The older man unfurled a handkerchief, wiping the rim of the barrel as he spoke. "I'm sorry, young master Kempf; but the decision was made the moment I gave you this name. There is no going back now..."

"That conviction, it's what separates us, you know?" he said, beating Martin down to the ground with a smack of the butt of the luger, "that specific defect in you is what brought us here today, actually."

The doctor prowled in a circle around Martin as he spoke, the young man groaning in pain. "I didn't think you'd get muddled up in a frenzy about jews of all things. I thought you were... bigger than that. I thought you'd see the führer's fierceness, his grandeur and scope of vision."

"I thought you'd see what he did to ascend to power, to seize authority from the remains of weaker minds and narrow, timid thinkers. Tonight, my vision for a future world order shall be fulfilled. Metropolis is in ruins, and my trusted lieutenants are scouring the Capitol for any remaining signs of resistance."

"Still… I had hoped that at least one of these prodigies would yield a worthy heir as the next of my line; the next Legion. No matter. Now that you are all cleaned up, at least I can divert my attention to other, more important things."

"Goodbye, Martin Kempf. Your life was squandered, and you will die in agony, alone and unloved, never seeing the masterpiece I shall create from the ashes of this so-called Ethocracy. What a pity." Dr. Anagonye concluded.

Folding his spectacles back onto the crook of his nose, Legion exited the graveyard briskly, disappearing into the life-world beyond.

§XXIB

When the doctor had vanished completely, Corvin appeared from a pocket of light which protruded from a nearby tree. Seeing the state of Martin, the All-Father clamored to sit by his side.

"Who are you?" Martin coughed.

"A friend." Corvin replied tearfully. "Though I'm afraid not friend enough it seems. You will die from these wounds Martin. I am sorry."

Martin was shaking. "I just— wanted to stop hurting people. Do you think," he sputtered, coughing up blood. "Do you think rabbi Heschel… that the congregants really forgave me?"

Corvin nodded. "Yes, he did. When he finds you in the morning, much grief will follow, and you shall be buried here."

Martin moaned briefly, tears welling across the sides of his face. "I hope so. How do you know?"

The All-Father held him. "I know a lot of things, child. For instance, I know why you come to this grave every day."

"The woman buried here… she is in you. You were her, in a former life. In part, you have relived out the experience of her trauma, and having found grace, you have healed a cycle of pain which once spiraled through uncountable generations. It only takes one, and that one was you Martin. Thank you."

Corvin touched the headstone. "Just as once you were her," he said, moving his hand to Martin's heart, "and for now you are here; soon you will be a child again—and the young are eternally the hope of all humankind. The past lives on always in the future, but the future is a force which heals. It will be okay, Martin. You have done well. All that is left is to stand the pain, and I shall be here for you until the end."

Martin looked tenderly in Corvin's eyes. "Actually, if it's the same to you, I think I'm okay alone… It feels right somehow."

The All-Father nodded, "Of course," he said, "but if you call out into the night, I will return. Rest easy, Martin Kempf." And with that, Corvin whisped away like the fog which pervaded the cemetery air.

Martin placed his blood-stained hand against the face of the tombstone with a meek smile. "So I guess we're the same again." he said gently. "Maybe it'll be okay someday for us, huh? Maybe… maybe it will be alright this time."

And then he faded out into that forever beyond, the words of the headstone lingering in the last enminded expression of that being called Martin Kempf.

Ashley Lanning
May 31, 2189—May 27, 2219
May her Memory be Always a Blessing

"Two things fill the mind with ever-increasing admiration and awe, the oftener and more steadily we reflect on them: the starry heavens above me and the moral law within me. I have not to search for them and conjecture them as though they were veiled in darkness or were in the transcendent region beyond my horizon; I see them before me and connect them directly with the consciousness of my existence."

— Immanuel Kant, *The Critique of Practical Reason*

§XXIIA

"At this point, we have to assume she's not coming back. I'm sorry Thea." Leveigh offered. His eyepatch was in the traditional black silk, and he sat in a wheelchair as they visited in the infirmary ward of the hospital. The lights were off, but people were everywhere, and the medical staff ran about them in the halls with a hasty exigence.

"I know." Thea replied with a vacant stare. "I just don't know what we do without her."

Leveigh nodded cautiously. "Well, in her absence, the Vanguard seems to be looking to you for guidance. So, we just have to figure out what you want to do, and do it."

Flight Officer Beckett nodded. "Have you been hearing the word on the ground that I have?" Corporal Simoneau blinked as Thea continued.

"Flight reports indicate a man of enormous stature, cloaked in shadow, sitting on a throne in the middle of the old Ringstrasse. Tentative ID is the Ravenous Thane, but now he is inhumanely large and suffused with some unidentified technology or... something like Oni... or Corvin. It's not clear."

Shakespeare entered the room. "You think it's connected: Oni disappearing, and suddenly he shows up all decked-out, magical and whatnot?" she asked.

Thea shrugged. "Who's to say? I've stopped pretending to have any idea of what's going on, and we're in no state to run a substantive intelligence operation right now. If we make it through this, I think the Vanguard will have to commission a team to investigate the matter further, but that's... well, let's not get ahead of ourselves."

As she said this, Dawud Makgoba walked in, wearing a K10 Theta flight-suit. "Good evening," he greeted. "Still feels strange, to wear this... It doesn't feel like I've earned it. Are you sure this is what you want Thea?"

"Listen," Flight Officer Beckett replied, "Oni Anagonye had limitless trust in you, Dawud. Though you may not have been elected, you are needed. But you have to understand: we are going into an extremely dangerous situation. You've already brushed with death once this week. Are you sure you're ready to do it again?"

Leveigh stood up shakily. "We're a crack team consisting of a guy who just got shot in the head, another who was crushed under a building, the woman whose spouse literally disappeared from right in front of her after committing mass murder, and a masterful 16th century playwright. What could possibly go wrong?"

They all looked at him wide-eyed. "I mean else." the Corporal explained. "What else could go wrong? I'm out of ideas. It seems like life has exhausted all the most obvious options. Might as well assume some things could go right now, yeah?"

Lieutenant von Goethe raised a finger. "Hmm… I mean, that's not rational in the strictest sense of the word, is it."

Leveigh leaned forward, placing the weight of his torso on his fists. "And what sense might that be, Bard of Avon?"

"The actual one," Shakespeare demurred, "also, point of order, shut up and stop calling me that." Leveigh laughed as von Goethe's grin bubbled reluctantly to the surface.

"That being said," the Lieutenant continued. "I hate to be frank, but if this was ever about conserving our livelihood, then the Vanguard never deserved to claim the mantle of an Ethocratic government anyways, right?" The new Watch of K10 Theta nodded in unison.

"Fair enough," Shakespeare said. "Then let's get to work. Oh and Thea?"

Flight Officer Beckett craned her neck.

"You're our Captain now. Got it? That's an order."

Thea nodded. A thin smile gleaned across her face before she resumed her sober demeanor.

"Alright then, K10 Theta. Let's get on with this."

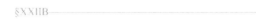

§XXIIB

The howling gale blew an ocean of mist across the barren valley. Oni barreled forwards, though the line of sight was obfuscated by the vapor which surrounded her.

"Oni?" Corvin's disembodied voice called out, surprised. "What are you doing here?"

Guarding her face against the elements, she yelled out in reply, "No idea, you tell me! I was in Metropolis one moment, and the next I'm wandering in this endless torrent. Where are we?"

Corvin appeared before her, guarding his face with the brim of his hat. With a wave of his hand, he created a forcefield barrier against the wind, which dulled and quieted the sound of the storm around them. A strange lightness permeated the space he created.

"We're in the stasis I created to entrap myself and the source of the shadow which has plagued me. I see in you that you've sensed its presence before… if you stay, we can meet him together and overcome the rift he has fostered in the world."

"But before we do, there is one quick thing to which I must attend." the All-Father explained. "Can you hold the shadow off for me? An old friend is dying. I will lay them to rest, and come right back."

Oni nodded. "Yeah," she reluctantly answered. "You need to go. Do it. I'll hold him."

"Thank you, friend." Corvin said, putting his hand on her shoulder. "Now, when I go, the being called El will confront you immediately. He's stronger than I thought, but I think he's still afraid to show himself with the two of us here. You need only survive until I return. I know you can do it. Do you trust me?"

"Yes," Oni replied, after which Corvin disappeared in a flurry of motion. Immediately, she felt a hand grasp the back of her neck. As the mist dissipated to reveal the oceanside of El's home, the embodiment of the dark flung her across the sand. As Oni regained her footing, the being called El drew his fingers across his face, revealing eyes where there had only been sockets before.

"Foolish girl." the voice of the shadow called out. "Don't you see how it's over? I've already won. Kill me here, if you can, but your world has already come undone. Though I may die, the dark will live on."

Oni charged the being called El, slamming her fist and elbow into his solar plexus, before striking his jaw square-on. As he staggered backwards gently, she struck him in the forehead, but as she returned her hand to deal another blow, he caught her fist in his, bending it slowly until the bones cracked underneath the force of his will.

"I told Corvin, the mortals would be their own undoing." he growled, bashing her shattered fist with a swift blow before assailing her chest with a two-palmed ram. She flew across the beachside, El calling out after her.

"Leave them as the masters of their fates and they bring about a long night of misery all on their own. It would have been far better to have let them find their fate in peace. Their subjugation is the kindest send-off ours can give them."

Oni entered dæmon form, reviving her arm with a brush of blue flame-like wonder. She called back. "You lived as a man once, but the world is so very different from when you were in the world. You are wrong about them. The culture you knew did not understand how to appeal to human beings' better natures. It doesn't have to be this way."

Corvin reappeared, standing in the white light of his own god-essence. "You misunderstand your own thoughts, El," the younger called out.

"The future of the world unfurls from lower to higher orders of complexity. You were right that human beings do great harm to themselves, but they also hold in them the birthright of the stars which are Our progeny."

"The things which are the pinnacle of our making are only the foundation to all of which they are capable. They are the future, not us.

We must let them grow, and help them in the process. We are meant to be their guardians, not their masters. It is they who are Sovereign over us, not the other way around."

El's crooked grin met the emergence of a dark energy which pulsed around him like a halo of poisoned blood. His eyes pooled with shadow as he started walking towards Corvin and Oni menacingly. "That is our choice to make, Fallen one. And as the chiefest among us, I refuse." And with that, he blasted forward, charging the two dæmon with perturbing force.

§XXII§

The Vanguard had surrounded the courtyard at the center of the Ringstrasse. As they marched, the Florentine Commission simply retreated until reaching the presence of the Ravenous Thane. There, they stood rank-and-file, an open column laid ready to approach the throne where Senator Wilson sat.

Thea and the members of K10 Theta approached solemnly toward the ceasefire, and as they reached the mouth of the runner ahead of them, the Ravenous stood from his seat.

He looked largely the same as before, though he had chosen to wear his mask in leisure. The greatest of disparities were vested in his stature, which was about four yards in height. Proportionately, he seemed bulky and athletic as before, but his body was cloaked in shadow, just as had been the case with Corvin.

Heathrow dismounted his seat, stepping towards Thea with a metered gait as he unsheathed the Quantic blade, now also swollen to several meters in length.

His voice bellowed with perilous intent, still distorted by the mechanisms of his suit. "Three hundred new volunteers for the grave. Or does the Vanguard now seek our mercy?"

Thea replied, undaunted. "We seek no refuge from the turncoats of the Prometheus."

Heathrow laughed, collapsing his helmet. "You misunderstand." he said plainly. "We *are* Prometheus. Though the Vanguard hoped to withhold all power from the nations, we, the Ravenous, gave them fire with which to burn you. And now they reign supreme."

"No longer do they bear the stain of your slur—these 'Machiavellians' are ascendant. They *are* the Senate. They are the rightful heirs of the State. And you and your precious von Galen shall hold no domain but that which belongs to the dead."

Shakespeare whispered. "Oni, if you're out there… We could really use your help about right the fuck now please."

"Seconded," Leveigh motioned. When Shakespeare gave him the strange-eye, Leveigh rebutted. "Generic plights can be seconded. Don't give me that look."

"Hey K10?" Thea whispered. Leveigh and Shakespeare attuned their gaze. When nothing followed, they each quietly nodded before shutting up.

"Alright, Vanguards." Thea announced over the Porta-COM tech. "Look sharp. Execute operation Yellow Vest in three… two… one…"

§XXIID

The dæmon barraged El from every angle. The dark god floated some ten meters off the ground, and blow after glancing blow struck him. Yet with every bombardment, he leered with newfound ferocity, and with increasing frequency managed to castigate them punishingly into the ground or ocean waves.

"This is not your battleground," El cried out after launching them together into the sand, which flung out as if parted by a meteor. He blasted them with a dark and twisted energy, and they screamed as it writhed around their forms, cutting and bleeding them. "No matter what you do, I will overcome you," said the olden one.

Corvin took Oni's hand as the azure brightness of her essence evaporated the sorcerous manacles which had ensnared them, at the same time relieving them of their wounds. El called out again. "You are weak. If this is how you wish to spend the rest of Eternity, caught up with me: so be it. Seeing your flashes of pain is satisfaction enough."

Again they collided, exchanging blows with electric repetition. Every explosion of light only glanced the being called El, who shifted wherever their light failed to go. Seeing this, Oni sought to grapple the Dark one and irradiate him, but as her being came up as if to touch him; she rebounded in agony. She sank towards the ocean for a moment. Then, shaking her head, she launched back towards her enemy.

Seconds before impact, Corvin intersected her, portaling the two of them away. El seethed, firing a wall of eldritch darkness towards them. The All-Father raised his hand, a comet of gold light shielding them from the attack. Though El persisted, and as time lingered, the tail of the protective ball thinned.

"He's right," Corvin yelled out, wincing in pain. "We cannot win, and we cannot escape. If we keep going like this, we're doomed."

"We can't just give up Corvin! We have to keep fighting!" Oni shouted back.

The All-Father nodded. "I know, but something has to change. Now I'm going to do what needs to be done, and I don't think you're going to like it, but it's the only way I can see for this to end the way we need it to. Take my hand!" he said urgently, and she obliged.

"Now listen to me," he continued. "On the count of three, I'm going to release this shield and take the full force of El's dark energy. It's enough to obliterate me, but my essence of the Light will be dispersed."

"At that moment, as long as we remain in contact, you will become one with the full force of the Light as it was in me. Now I was also infected with the dark, and even with my share I don't think you'll be fully godhead, but neither is he. I'm not actually sure what he is… but the power you'll gain may just be enough to overcome him."

Oni's eyes widened. "No, Corvin—you can't. I've lost too many people already. I can't lose you. I haven't had a chance to say this yet but… I'm really scared. I'm not like myself lately. I need your help. I'm not good at this like you are."

Corvin shook his head. "Oni, it has been an honor to even know you. You will make it through this, I am sure of it. I love you, friend. And a part of me will never forget you," he smiled. "One… Two…"

"Corvin please!" Oni cried.

" Three."

<hr>

§XXIII

Captain's Log, September 23rd, 2219

Operation Yellow Vest had seemed to fail. When first we charged, the Ravenous Thane swept his own soldiers out of existence with a brush of his fingers. The sight of his eyes, just as he did so… It was like he relished the thought of extinguishing human life by his own hand however indiscriminately. I've never seen such a sinister look in my life… and I hope I never do again.

The Vanguard was swift and courageous. We all swarmed him together, in waves. Many of us expected to die, and at the time it seemed as though many of us did. His mastery of the weapon alone was not enough to explain how quickly he eviscerated our assault. It was as if his hand were possessed of a spirit whose sole purpose was the destruction of the Vanguard.

Suffice it to say, no one got close enough to plant explosives, and our rockets were ineffective. In desperation, some Vanguards moved to pick up errant guns left from the Machiavellians, but they too were obviously useless. The details of the casualties were unclear in the moment. I had been cleaved by the Thane's Quantic blade early in the assault, and had anticipated my own death to follow.

It was when I collapsed on the ground, bleeding out on the cobblestone path, that the strangest visage came before me. A wall of blue fire, as tall as glaciers, swam like an ocean towards the old Ringstrasse. Leading its course was… a woman, or the shape of a woman. She was some ways off, but I felt as though I could see her.

She gleamed like starlight, and her kinky tresses of hair seemed to shimmer like sunbeams as she walked. Her eyes were like boulders of sapphire caught in the unvarnished light of all the Cosmos, and for a second she gazed right at me. Now, empirically there is nothing I can say for certain, but it is my utmost conviction that the person I saw was the Commander Oni Anagonye, to whom this Captain is betrothed to marry, and who has been missing in action since the events leading up to that fateful day.

The being lifted up her hand, and the flames poured into herself. Progressively, her energy came to illuminate the whole city with a blinding radiance; the sort of light you imagine when the words hydrogen and bomb come together in a sentence. And then, emanating from her body was this great… lance of azure energy which shot into the Ravenous Thane. He screamed loud enough to fill the corridors of every street. As this beam pierced him, it seemed like parts of his body flaked off of his person, and when the light dimmed he was down to his normal size and self—the shadow completely cast out of him. As this happened, she rose into the air before seeming to pour out into the fixed point of every star in the sky. And then she was gone.

But the Thane survived, and he stood up, Quantic blade in-hand. My soldiers were ready to confront him, but I was not about to lose anyone else that day. And so we retreated, which I still consider to be the best decision of my career—for as we left and found a fuller view of the city, many dozens of Florentines with Quantic weaponry could be seen closing in, clamoring to the defense of their wounded master.

We still have much to learn about the workings of the new Machiavellian order, though now they go by a different name as some sort of symbol of their heightened legitimacy—calling themselves simply 'the Prometheans.' Whatever the case, I am convinced that we have yet to unearth the full scale of their operation, and that doing so will be crucial to overcoming them.

Some things have changed as a result of these events in terms of the constitutionality of our government. Firstly, anyone may work to claim the entitlements of 'Vanguard' by birthright now. This is partly a matter of practicality (as we have lost so many), and partly an alteration from necessity. Everyone must serve the full duties of the Vanguard if they would like to lay claim to political authority;—we suspect that the unaccountable privileging of 'Senator' status likely made the Prometheus vulnerable to corruption.

And finally, we have decided to allow no more essential government facilities in space. As Corporal Leveigh put it, "it's time to live a bit more down-to-Earth." And so we have our peacekeeping operations running through Three Waters, Scotland, and the commerce capital in Prague— a decision made in honor of our Commander, who had grown quite in love with its community, history, and charm.

Metropolis remains occupied by hostile forces, and our intelligence indicates that it is quickly descending into a full authoritarian state. The media, the policing. All of it. Until we have liberated every last survivor in that city, it is safe to say we have failed our mission.

I am a poor substitute for Oni Anagonye, but in her absence, I will not hesitate to lead our cause through whatever we may face. Long may the Vanguard live,

forever for humanity.
Thea Mae Beckett
Captain of the Vanguard

"Too many of today's mainline Protestants spend more time seeking out the likes of Hobbes and Rand for their political wisdom than actual Christians like More, Tillich, Moltmann, Bonhoeffer, Volf, or—you know—Jesus. If these Christians were actually for Christ, then these morbidly pessimistic evaluations of human nature and human dignity would be anathema to them."

"The Ethocracy has been implicit in the narratives of serious Christian thinkers long before von Galen was around. We were the first socialists, the first ethocrats, and will continue to anticipate the eschatological unfolding of a just society on earth; and it is on this account that the deeper truths of the Christian religion stake their validity in prescribing the just society. Were a godless utopia possible, there would be no need for belief."

- Catherine Decker, *instructor of political theology at the Harvard Divinity School*

One Year Later

§XXIIIA

Prague's Cathedral of Saint Vitus was bathed in prisms of light. Vegetation sprawled across the whole view, admixed with a flutter of songbirds and other small fauna.

The cathedral was converted into a porous space, blurring the lines between outside and in, and there were no pews. In their stead, children of various ages sat in small clusters around each stained glass, helmed by Vanguards who engaged their audiences in dialogue; books at their side and smiles situated on bright faces.

The windows themselves had been transformed—where once there were icons to saints and apostles, each frame now adorned the sight of figures of a different sort; the subjects of discussion aligning with each depiction.

The likenesses of Einstein and Christa McAuliffe perched between the passionate rendering of stars; Anscombe and Wittgenstein reading intently in a library; Marx and Martin Luther King Jr. at the head of a temple with great sequoia-like pillars perching a magnificent arch above; Maya Angelou and Franz Kafka sitting at a picnic by a river.

"I lobbied to have one made after your namesake, you know." Leveigh said to the Lieutenant, "the Bard and Goethe, back to back buddy-cop style like in those 20th century shoestring budget TV specials."

Von Goethe turned her face to him with a diagonal stare. "You best be careful beau—I've dropkicked men out of my life for less."

Leveigh blushed. "Yes, well, I suppose I'll have to make it up to you somehow… do you think designing a stain glass window in your honor would count?"

Shakespeare hummed in thought. "I think I'll settle for you not doing that instead. Deal?"

The Corporal kissed her cheek in reply. "Deal," he answered softly, as they both returned their gaze to the artwork in front of them.

"You know," she whispered, "I really love these. And this practice of turning sacred spaces into learning gardens… this was von Galen's idea?"

Leveigh nodded. "Yes, it comes from his lesser known *Treatise on Education*. In it, he talks about Augustine's conception of virtue as 'rightly-ordered love', and sought to remind society that as our consciousness of love is elevated, so too must our institutions rise."

"His philosophy of education sought to dismantle the productivity-narrative of the nation-state, understanding that the act of exchanging ideas is an end in itself worthy of the monuments of our greatest affection. That humanity and its joy is the object for which all the work of Civilization must labor."

The Lieutenant's eyes grew large. "I didn't know you were so intimately familiar with von Galen's whole corpus."

"Well," Leveigh replied with a grin and a shrug, "you try sharing every moment with Oni Anagonye without familiarizing yourself with the philosopher's entire known works. It doesn't bode well for you, I'll tell you what." after a moment, his smile shrunk.

"Oni…" Shakespeare drifted. The two Vanguards turned to face the far end of the Cathedral, where Thea sat at her desk, fervently scribbling away on a bundle of paper. Their eyes met, and Leveigh nodded. Then, they briskly jogged up the length of the foyer to greet her.

"How's the manuscript coming along?" von Goethe inquired.

Thea looked up at her partners. "Oh, you know… it's a process. It gets developed bit by bit as my duties give space for a moment on occasion."

Corporal Simoneau's face brightened. "Hey, that's really great! So many things have come to pass—the public needs to hear an account of it from someone they can trust, who saw it themselves. There's so much to discuss… I can't wait to see what you've written."

Thea sighed.

"Hey, Thea. I'm sorry she's still missing." said Shakespeare, "I think you're right that she was responsible for that phenomena that saved us back in Old Wien. She's out there. We'll see her again. You have to believe that."

The Captain looked into her folded hands as she rolled the ring along her finger. "I know." she said, dry-eyed. Lines wore across her sunken cheeks, but a soft smile still lingered as she nodded to her companions.

"I know."

The faint sound of rainfall caressed the holy grounds, and on the far end of the building, Thea caught sight of Dawud Makgoba walking out the exit as he unfurled a multicolored umbrella.

She stood up. "If you'll excuse me." she said quietly. Her colleagues nodded and bowed out of her way as she left the platform of the atrium.

§XXIIIB

Walking briskly, she caught Dawud standing there, looking skywards, in enjoyment of the water as it fell.

"Hey rookie!" Thea called out. "The shield of the flight-suits eliminates the need for an umbrella. You don't have to use one of those."

Dawud nodded. "Oh, I know. All the same, I'm rather fond of it... Are you leaving for the day as well? We could catch a cab together!" he called out as the gentle tapping of the sky-fall essence bloomed into a full-on downpour.

"Actually," Thea replied. "I'm heading up to HQ in Glen Coe in a moment. I'm afraid the conflict with the Prometheans will soon spill over into a global conflict. Their consolidation of power has become complete, and they're mobilizing to increase their territorial hold of Western Europe already. Soon we will have to announce to the public that we are a world at war."

"I think they mostly know already," said Dawud, "but it will be good for people to hear it from you."

Thea nodded with a subdued composure.

"How are you holding up?" Dawud asked.

257

"Good." the Captain replied. "I'm doing well. Thanks for asking."

Dawud frowned. "It's okay to not be doing well Thea. Your partner is missing, and it's unclear when you might see her again. You've lost friends, colleagues, and your life has become a whirlwind of difficulties... And, it is only natural to be pained at her absence."

Thea shook her head modestly. "No, it's not like that."

Dawud's brow shifted as he gazed attentively at his friend.

"She's not absent to me. She's everywhere." Thea Mae Beckett replied. "All these Vanguards who are still alive, the progress of Ethocratic theory, the well-being of the city which we now call home... Her heart was in all of it, and without her none of this would have been possible... It's hard to explain what the difficulty is."

Dawud gave Thea a hug. "Words can only take us so far. But that feeling you have... it dwells within me too."

He took her hands in his. "That's why we all have each other. No need to explain. No demands. Just love."

"Just love?" Thea's face brightened as the sky broke open. "I can get behind that."

In the Shadow
of Prometheus

the Saga will Continue in Book Two,
Visions of a Spirit Seer
with your help!

See the last page for details,

and don't forget to visit
www.theringsaga.com

Author Bio

L. Farnsworth Colson lives in Ithaca, NY alongside his partner Kieren and their wonderful pug-beagle 'puggle' mix Brody.

His passion for storytelling began in grade school, making Whedon-inspired films with childhood friends and short stories for the amusement of his classmates.

While in high school, he cut his teeth on the writings of Shakespeare of Avon, C.S. Lewis, Ray Bradbury, Susanna Clarke, J.K Rowling, Terry Pratchett, Neil Gaiman, and Philip Pullman—influences which would later come to shape the aesthetic tastes of his own literary style.

During his undergraduate years, he became enamored of the format of the philosophical novel—particularly embracing Dostoyevsky, Kafka, Nietzsche, and Kierkegaard. Then, Colson undertook a robust study of the philosophy of Immanuel Kant—an enquiry which cemented his intellectual priorities and fundamentally transformed his views of the world, society, and experience.

Receiving his bachelor's degree in the New Hampshire University System as president of the history honors society, L. Farnsworth attended Yale for his graduate studies in the philosophy of religion. Somewhere in all of that, he swears he must have heard something useful, and promises to get back to you with the details...

More seriously — growing tired of the insularity of the academy and concerned with the injustices perpetuated at home and abroad, the author of Prometheus delayed his doctoral studies in pursuit of creating a story which could welcome a larger audience into the philosophical ideas that have come to fundamentally shape our civilization over the course of its history.

L. Farnsworth Colson enjoys drinking exceptional coffee, reading academic monographs of dubious merit, and petting cats despite the strong protestations of his allergist. You will find him alternately canvassing for the 2020 election in the wider tristate area, or else sitting in an affordable foodie joint with good friends and a great lunch.

You can keep up with his writing efforts at www.theringsaga.com

One Final Note

Plato taught us that ultimately, the purpose of philosophy is preparation for death. I quite agree, and have found the literature to be a salve for my own edification.

And yet, there are limits to what reason can tell us about the After, and so we are left to strain with great anxiety about what to make of the inevitable extirpation of our selfhood from the world. I have made several hints about my own position on the ontology of Life in *Prometheus*, and I won't repeat them here. However, there is more to say, and at least some of it would be timely to reflect on as we close out this book.

The eminent and remarkable comedian Hannah Gadsby cautioned us against the conventional thought that it is the *duty* of artists to suffer. Yet sit down with an artist, and you will invariably find in them the personality of one who has suffered tremendously. Much of that is completely reducible to their humanity. No matter what your walk in life: being a person is *hard* work.

But for artists, suffering often extends from the experience of a trauma or traumas so profound that ordinary speech is no longer sufficient; the project of creativity becomes the only remaining consolation in the world. Not all who suffer so profoundly are artists, and there are some artists who do not suffer so profoundly, and yet—there is something about the drive to bring new meaning into the world that is peculiarly strong in those who have seen unfathomable destruction.

Now none of this should be taken to mean that I wish to speak to artists at the exclusion of others. It means that as an artist, and as someone who has likewise struggled, I want to use my platform and my voice to express solidarity with those who feel overwhelmed by this pain.

And I am no professional when it comes to the work of supporting people through such strife, so all I can say is that even if we have never met, and no matter who you are —I love you, I care that you are with us, and your life matters to me. The more you've lacked these things in your own experience, the more urgent it is to me that you internalize what I am saying, because I've been there. I know that gestures like this can feel insincere in the moment. But it's how I feel. I promise you.

Nevertheless, since I am not a mental health worker: no matter how urgently I feel the need for you to be taken care of, I know that I am not the best-equipped to do it— fortunately, there exists free and reliable access to people who are.

If you feel like you're out of options, please contact your local crisis/support hotline. If you are an American, the number is 1-800-273-8255. If this avenue will not work for you, please visit www.iasp.info to find the assistance you require. Help is out there.

For whatever ways in which this book or any of my efforts surrounding it have been life-affirming, they should be taken as memorial to the life and love of Edward Charles Burke, my partner's uncle who died of suicide last summer. I regret that I never had the opportunity to meet him, but his family has been a beacon of joy and warmth to me ever since I first came to their doorstep. I know some of that light was his, and I will endeavor to pass along its brightness to as many other candles as my own reach allows.

To everyone reading—be well, live long, and know that no matter what you think you deserve or believe is possible: you are loved. If truly by no one else (though this is most often believed erroneously), then at the very least by me. More than a thousand hours went into the making of this book, and every single one of them was undertaken with you in mind, dear friend.

Despite how it may feel right now: it truly does get better, and this too shall pass. All manner of things will pass. And the world turns, with every spin bringing light and warmth and joy and play to the endlessly beautiful and tenacious thing we call Life. And it's better with you there. At least for me it is.

Forever with you,

L. Farnsworth Colson

L. Farnsworth Colson

Many hundreds of hours of work went into the writing of this manuscript, and a similar amount of time and money went into the production of its contents in this present form. The work was a labor of love by all.

If you would like to help facilitate the creation of its sequels, please consider supporting the artists who made it possible by spreading the word, sharing this story, and following & financing their efforts.

L. Farnsworth Colson

Twitter - twitter.com/LFarnsworthCol

Facebook - facebook.com/LFarnsworthColson

Patreon - patreon.com/LFarnsworth

John Sumrow —

Twitter - twitter.com/sumrow

Facebook - facebook.com/sumrow

Patreon - patreon.com/JohnSumrow

Raven Gill —

Facebook - facebook.com/RavenGillDesign

Behance - behance.net/RavenGill

if you have enjoyed this novel
tweet, post, share media and
let your peers know that
#Prometheus and
#TheRingSaga
are worth their time

a dozen more stories
such as this can be told

but only with your help

Made in the USA
Middletown, DE
03 May 2019